The One I Love

WATASHI NO SUKINAHITO

わたしのすきなひと

BY

CLAMP

TOKYOPOP®

HAMBURG // LONDON // LOS ANGELES // TOKYO

NANASE OHKAWA STORY・ESSAY

WATASHI NO SUKINA HITO

SCENE 3・AITAI 027
SCENE 4・TOSHISHITA 037
SCENE 7・KIREI 069
SCENE 8・FUAN 079
SCENE 11・HANARERU 109
SCENE 12・KEKKON 119

COMIC MICK NEKOI

SCENE 6・ISSHONI 059
SCENE 9・YÛKI 089
SCENE 10・FUTSÛ 099
SCENE 1・CHIGAU 005
SCENE 5・TOTSUZEN 049
SCENE 2・KAWAII 015

W A T A S H I N O S U K I N A H I T O

STAFF

COMIC 猫井みっく

MICK NEKOI

STORY・ESSAY 大川七瀬

NANASE OHKAWA

DESIGN／SATSUKI IGARASHI
NANASE OHKAWA

SPECIAL THANKS／MOKONA APAPA
KAKYOU

TODAY I WORE A KIMONO.
I PUT IT ON BY MYSELF, SO IT MIGHT LOOK A LITTLE WEIRD.
BUT I DID MY BEST TO WEAR IT.
SCENE1 Different
I WANTED TO TRY SOMETHING A LITTLE DIFFERENT, TO BECOME A LITTLE DIFFERENT.

MAYBE IT WAS MY FAULT AFTER ALL...
WE HAD A FIGHT A WEEK AGO.
IT WAS OVER SOMETHING SMALL.
BUT BOTH HE AND I WERE STUBBORN AND I COULDN'T SAY THE TWO WORDS THAT MATTERED.
I'M SORRY.
......
OHH, IT'S SO EASY TO SAY WHEN HE'S NOT HERE...
Hic...
She's a weirdo.
Sure is.
BUT... YOU'RE TO BLAME TOO.
AFTER WE FOUGHT, IF YOU HAD ONLY...
IF YOU HAD SMILED, EVEN A LITTLE...I COULD HAVE BEEN A LITTLE MORE HONEST, INSTEAD OF STUBBORN.

I HATE FIGHTING.
BUT I HATE HOLDING MY FEELINGS IN EVEN MORE.
THE LONGER I HOLD THEM IN, THE DEEPER THE NEGATIVE FEELINGS SEEP INTO MY HEART.
AND THOSE NEGATIVE FEELINGS IGNITE A SPARK THAT EXPLODES INSIDE ME, AND THEN IT BECOMES MORE THAN JUST A LITTLE ARGUMENT.
AND THEN...
...THINGS END...
AT LEAST, THAT'S HOW IT FEELS...
I WANT TO APOLOGIZE. I WANT TO TELL YOU THAT I'M SORRY.
BUT IT'S HARD TO SAY WHAT I FEEL...
SO INSTEAD...
...I WORE A KIMONO TODAY.

I WANTED TO BE DIFFERENT TODAY, SO I WOKE UP EARLY AND PUT ON A KIMONO.
I'VE ALWAYS FELT DIFFERENT IN A KIMONO.
MY MOTHER HAS SCOLDED ME FOR BEING AGITATED...
BUT SOMEHOW, IN A KIMONO, I'M AT PEACE, EVEN WHEN PERFORMING MY LESSONS. I HOPE THAT...
...IF I CAN BECOME DIFFERENT IN A KIMONO, I CAN ALSO BECOME HONEST.

B-BUT, WHAT IF I DON'T LOOK GOOD IN THIS KIMONO?!
I WAS SAVING THIS ONE FOR A SPECIAL OCCASION, SO I'VE NEVER WORN IT, NOT EVEN TO CHECK AND MAKE SURE I LOOK GOOD IN IT!
バタ バタ
OH! MAYBE I SHOULD HAVE WORN THE RED ONE!
Oh great, some freak's causing a scene...
OR MAYBE THE LIGHT BLUE ONE!
WHOA!!
ドッカン
I'M SORRY!

OH...
Oh... It's you...
W-WHY ARE YOU DRESSED LIKE THAT? YOU ALWAYS WEAR JEANS.
Same jeans every day.
Yawn

END

SCENE·1/CHIGAU

(Different) ちがう

Hello. This is CLAMP. For those of you wondering who we are, let me explain. CLAMP is a collective of four people—Satsuki Igarashi, Nanase Ohkawa, Mick Nekoi, and Mokona Apapa. We have created and produced several manga.

This project, *The One I Love,* is a collection of essays centered around girls' love and the insecurity, happiness, regret, and satisfaction that accompanies that love.

Each chapter includes seven pages of manga illustrated by Mick Nekoi and a short essay section written by me, Nanase Ohkawa. We hope you enjoy this journey through love.

WATASHI NO SUKINAHITO
わたしのすきなひと

Have you ever wanted to become someone different? I know I have. Mostly, I feel like turning into someone else when I'm either disgusted with myself or thoroughly depressed. Sometimes I find myself thinking: *How could I have been so stupid? If there were a ditch I'd jump into it.* Or... *What was I thinking when I said that?!*

So this story is based on an experience I had. It wasn't a romantic experience (too bad, right?), but rather an incident between a friend and myself. She and I go way back and have been friends for about fifteen years. But three years ago, I had an argument with her. And it was over something insignificant.

Usually, we laugh off stuff like that—but at that time—we couldn't. We must have been tired after endless all-nighters. (I bet you're wondering why all the all-nighters. Too bad, keep on wondering.)

Anyway, most of the time my friend and I are courteous of each other's feelings, but for some reason when we parted that day, neither of us felt good about our exchange. After agonizing over our "fight" for a week, I decided I wanted to apologize to her, so I called and asked her to meet me. Of course, there was no guarantee that things wouldn't go terribly wrong, again.

I ended up wearing a kimono to our rendezvous. I figured that if I changed who I was maybe it would change the outcome. I guess, the more you love someone, the harder it is to say you're sorry.

So, whenever you have a hard time apologizing—remember this story. If you can become someone different than the person who had the fight, you might be able to deal with the situation a bit more honestly.

By the way, the day I wore that kimono, my friend wore her choir uniform! (great minds think alike) And thankfully, she is still one of my best friends.

SCENE2 Cute
I THINK CUTE IS SUCH A VAGUE WORD.
I CAN SORT OF UNDERSTAND BEAUTIFUL, BUT I HAVE A HARD TIME ACCEPTING CUTE.
YET...
IT'S REALLY HARD TO ACCEPT THE WORD CUTE.
WHY?
I CAN UNDERSTAND BEAUTIFUL.
I CAN SORT OF VISUALIZE IT.

OKAY.
BUT CUTE IS JUST TOO VAGUE.
YOU THINK?
THE WORD CUTE IS JUST SO GENERAL. I MEAN, YOU CAN USE IT TO MEAN ANYTHING.
Keep Our School Clean
THAT FLOWER'S CUTE.
THAT BIRD'S CUTE.
THAT MAN-HOLE'S CUTE.
YOU THINK A MAN-HOLE'S CUTE?
DIFFERENT STROKES FOR DIFFERENT FOLKS. BUT IT'S NOT AS STRANGE AS SAYING THAT MANHOLE'S BEAUTIFUL, RIGHT?
WELL, I DON'T THINK THERE ARE TOO MANY PEOPLE WHO WOULD CALL A MANHOLE...
...BEAUTIFUL, BUT I'M SURE SOMEBODY SOMEWHERE WOULD CALL A MANHOLE CUTE, RIGHT?
YOU THINK?
I DO.

FOR INSTANCE, WHEN I LOOK AT THIS MANHOLE, I THINK ABOUT HOW BRAVE AND CUTE IT IS.
THIS MAN-HOLE?
AFTER ALL, NO MATTER HOW MANY PEOPLE STEP ON IT, IT NEVER ONCE COMPLAINS.
WELL, YOU HAVE A POINT THERE.
I'VE NEVER THOUGHT *CUTE* HAD ANY SPECIAL MEANING.
WHEN PEOPLE DON'T KNOW HOW TO COMMENT ON SOMETHING, THEY USUALLY PRETEND THEY HAVE AN OPINION BY SAYING IT'S CUTE.
LIKE WHAT?
FOR EXAMPLE, WHEN A NEWLYWED COUPLE HAS THEIR FIRST BABY AND YOU LOOK AT IT, YOU SAY...
WHAT A CUTE BABY.
1
IF THE SCHOOL TRUSTEE WALKS HIS WHITE DOG ON CAMPUS, YOU SAY...
WHAT A CUTE DOG.
2
YOU'RE OUT SHOPPING, AND YOU SEE A PENGUIN DOLL IN THE DEPARTMENT STORE WINDOW, YOU SAY...
WHAT A CUTE PENGUIN.
3

SEE?
I SEE.
THAT'S WHY...
...I'VE ALWAYS SAID YOU CAN'T TRUST THE WORD *CUTE.*
FOR NINETEEN YEARS, I'VE SAID THIS OR THAT IS CUTE WHENEVER AND FOR WHATEVER.
SO WHEN SOMEONE TELLS ME THAT I'M CUTE...
...I ALWAYS FIGURE THAT THEY'RE JUST BEING PLEASANT AND MAKING CONVERSATION.

SOMEONE COULD TELL ME I'M CUTE, BUT I WOULDN'T GET HAPPY OR EXCITED ABOUT IT.
SO NO MATTER WHO SAYS THE WORD *CUTE*, NO MATTER THE SITUATION, I'VE NEVER BEEN PARTICULARLY IMPRESSED. YOU KNOW-- IN ONE EAR, OUT THE OTHER.
BUT...
WHY?
LATELY, I'VE CHANGED MY WAY OF THINKING, JUST A LITTLE.
WHAT DO YOU THINK OF ME?
くるん

YOU'RE CUTE.
すざざざざ
WHAT IS IT?
I CAN'T TAKE IT!
I DON'T UNDERSTAND! I DON'T FEEL ANYTHING WHEN ANYONE ELSE SAYS IT!
BUT SOMEHOW, WHEN YOU SAY I'M CUTE...
...MY HEART FLUTTERS.
ARE YOU OKAY? YOUR FACE IS ALL RED.
どき どき どき

I'M NOT OKAY, BUT...
I HOPE I CAN STAY EXCITED, LIKE THIS.
STRANGE, HUH?
HEY, YOU'RE LOOKING CUTE TODAY TOO!
SEE, NOTHING! I WONDER WHAT IT IS?
TAKE YOUR TIME AND THINK IT OVER.
'CAUSE I'LL TELL YOU HOW CUTE YOU ARE EVERY DAY FROM NOW ON.
ぽふん
AND I'LL BE CAREFUL THAT MY HEART DOESN'T EXPLODE FROM THE EXCITEMENT.

END

SCENE·2/KAWAII

(Cute) かわいい

The word *cute* really is very vague. I'm sure all of you have said the word *cute* recently. Like when you say: "What a cute little girl" or "That outfit is so cute."

Cute is such a convenient word. It can be used in all sorts of situations. I know I use *cute* more than four times a day, and yet, I don't even understand what it means entirely. I know the gist of it, but if you asked me to explain it in sixty words or less, I'd be hopelessly lost.

Long ago, I was involved in an incident involving the word *cute*. One of my relative's was getting married, and I was planning on wearing this adorable natural-fiber one-piece dress to the wedding. But that morning, I spilled milk on the dress, and had to wear a pink skirt instead.

WATASHI NO SUKINAHITO

わたしのすきなひと

I detested that pink skirt, just the *thought* of wearing it made me sad (yeah, yeah, I've always been a pretty simple person). The skirt looked so awful on me (or so I thought), and I felt like the most "un-cute" person in the world.

However, my uncles and aunts kept telling me how cute I looked in my skirt. And so, I became certain that *cute* was used as a social pleasantry. If you just say *cute,* you can gracefully survive even the most awkward of circumstances.

Maybe they really did think I looked cute, but since I was just a kid, I felt hurt when I realized the word *cute* could mean—cute, kinda cute, really cute, and "I have no idea what to say, so I'll just play it safe with *cute.*"

WATASHI NO SUKINAHITO
わたしのすきなひと

Even as an adult (although I'm still a kid inside), I don't understand what *cute* truly means.

Sometimes I feel as if it has some sort of special meaning, and sometimes I don't. When people tell me my accessories or my clothes are cute, it makes me happy. But on the other hand, they may not have meant anything special by it, and so getting giddy would be kind of out of line.

I used to try to think about the subtext behind the word, before I reacted to it. But recently, things have changed. Even though I have my doubts about *cute,* when a certain someone tells me I'm cute, I tend to lose my composure. I get all nervous and happy, and for that entire day, I feel like I'm on cloud nine.

I wonder why.

So, truth be told, this story is based on my own personal experience. Huh? You want to know who this person is? Well, maybe I'll tell you when it's just the two of us. But then again…sometimes things are better left unsaid.

WATASHI NO SUKINAHITO
わたしのすきなひと

WATASHI NO SUKINAHITO

わたしのすきなひと

I HAVE A LOVER.
A LOVER WHO I HARDLY EVER SEE.
SCENE3 I Miss You
HE'S A MANGA-KA WHO SPENDS MORE TIME WITH HIS DESK THAN ME.
BUT I'VE HAD ENOUGH.
IT'S HARD.
HE'S NOT ANSWERING THE PHONE AGAIN.

FINE, I CAN UNDERSTAND IF YOU DON'T WANT TO ANSWER THE PHONE BECAUSE YOUR EDITOR MIGHT BE ON THE LINE.
BUT WHAT IF IT'S ME?!
CAN'T YOU AT LEAST LEAVE YOUR ANSWERING MACHINE ON?! ASSHOLE!
ガチャン
I FEEL INSECURE WHEN I CAN'T SEE YOU.
ドスドス
WHEN I CAN'T SEE YOU, I DON'T KNOW IF SOMETHING'S HAPPENED TO YOU.
I DON'T KNOW IF YOU'RE WORKING, OR IF YOU'RE WITH SOMEONE ELSE.
I SHOULD WAIT OUTSIDE HIS OFFICE!
ONLY, THAT DOESN'T WORK. USUALLY, SOMEBODY'S ALREADY THERE.
ONCE, WHEN I COULDN'T GET IN TOUCH WITH HIM FOR THREE WEEKS, I FINALLY BROKE DOWN AND WENT TO HIS APARTMENT.
IT MUST BE TOUGH BEING AN EDITOR.

BUT...
...WE CONTINUE, AND I FIND MYSELF ABOUT TO UTTER A PHRASE LOATHED BY MEN FAR AND WIDE...
WHICH IS MORE IMPORTANT TO YOU, ME...
...OR YOUR WORK?
GUYS HAVE A TOUGH TIME WITH THAT LINE.
ALL THE MAGAZINES SAY THAT'S THE WORST THING A GIRL COULD SAY.
BUT STILL...
So should I leech off you, or just be poor?
That's so unfair! That's not what I meant...
WHAT ABOUT THE GIRL WHO FEELS SHE HAS TO SAY IT?

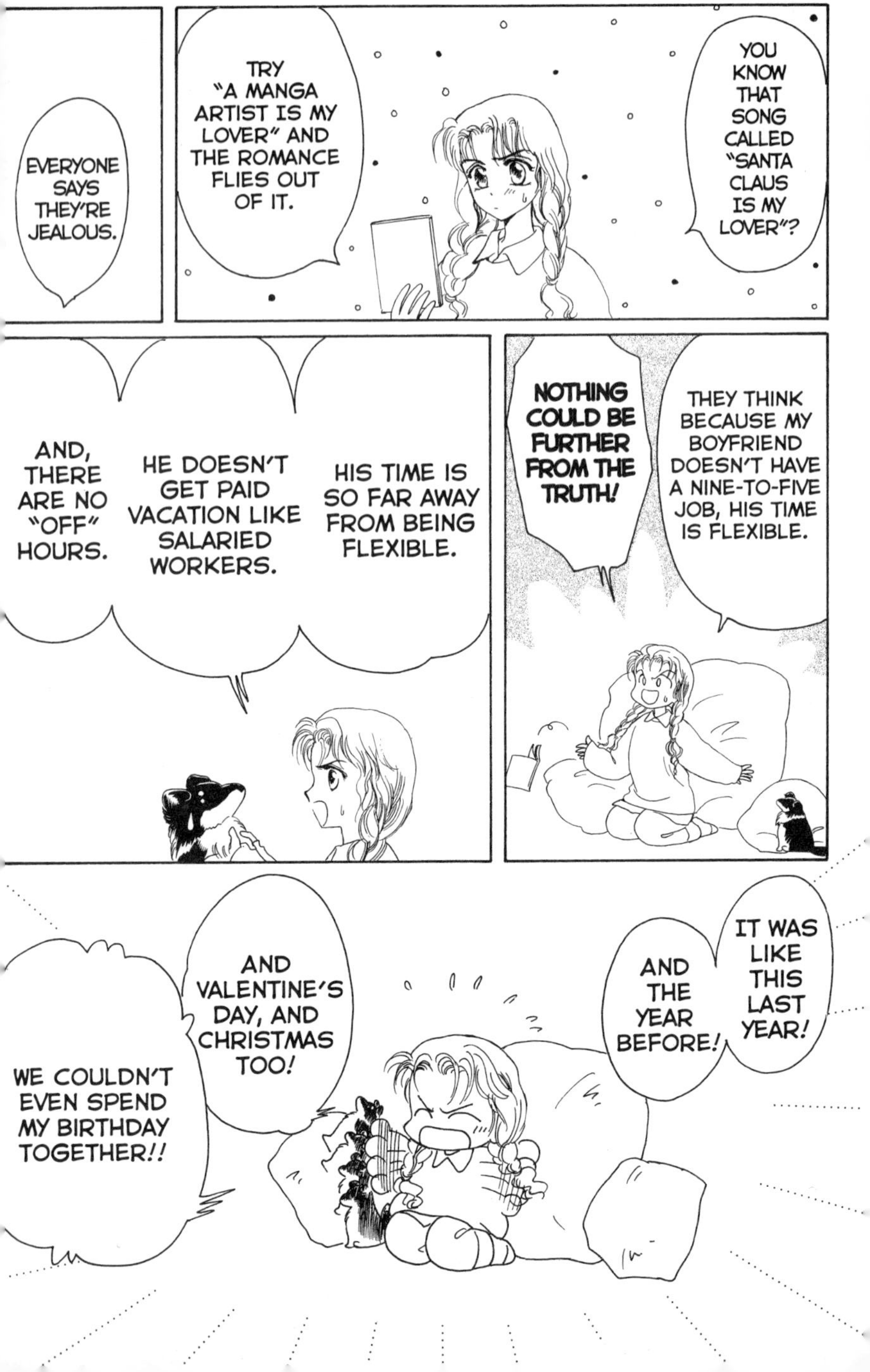
YOU KNOW THAT SONG CALLED "SANTA CLAUS IS MY LOVER"?
TRY "A MANGA ARTIST IS MY LOVER" AND THE ROMANCE FLIES OUT OF IT.
EVERYONE SAYS THEY'RE JEALOUS.
THEY THINK BECAUSE MY BOYFRIEND DOESN'T HAVE A NINE-TO-FIVE JOB, HIS TIME IS FLEXIBLE.
NOTHING COULD BE FURTHER FROM THE TRUTH!
HIS TIME IS SO FAR AWAY FROM BEING FLEXIBLE.
HE DOESN'T GET PAID VACATION LIKE SALARIED WORKERS.
AND, THERE ARE NO "OFF" HOURS.
IT WAS LIKE THIS LAST YEAR!
AND THE YEAR BEFORE!
AND VALENTINE'S DAY, AND CHRISTMAS TOO!
WE COULDN'T EVEN SPEND MY BIRTHDAY TOGETHER!!

I JUST WANT TO SEE HIM.
THAT'S ALL. NOTHING COMPLICATED.
FOR A GIRL...
...HAPPINESS IS BEING WITH THE ONE SHE LOVES.
はっ
ピンポーン
ピンポーン
ding-dong!
ding-dong!
OR AM I THE ONLY ONE WHO THINKS LIKE THAT...?
SHUT UP, ALREADY! I'M HAVING SOME PRODUCTIVE THOUGHTS HERE!
I'M NOT SUBSCRIBING TO ANY NEWSPAPERS OR MAGAZINES! AND I ALREADY HAVE CABLE!
カチャ

I'M SORRY. IT'S LATE.
UH, WERE YOU ABOUT TO GO TO BED?
SORRY, I'LL LEAVE SOON.
W-WHAT IS IT...?
I JUST WANTED TO SEE YOU.
HONESTLY, I HAVE A DEADLINE TOMORROW.
SO I DITCHED MY EDITOR AND CAME HERE.
BUT ALL OF A SUDDEN I HAD TO SEE YOU.
SORRY, I'LL LEAVE NOW.
WAIT.

HEY.
WHY DON'T YOU STAY AND HAVE A CAFÉ AU LAIT?
OKAY.
GUESS YOU WANTED TO SEE ME AS MUCH AS...
...I WANTED TO SEE YOU.
I'M SORRY TO BUG YOU WHEN YOU'RE BUSY.
BUT I SOMETIMES FEEL INSECURE.
SO PLEASE TRY TO VISIT ME WHEN YOU CAN.
AND I'M SORRY FOR HAVING THESE SILLY THOUGHTS.
BECAUSE THAT'S ALL I NEED TO BE THE HAPPIEST GIRL IN THE WORLD.
END

SCENE·3/AITAI

(I Miss You) あいたい

This story is based on a conversation CLAMP had with one of our few remaining friends, the manga-ka Okazaki Takeshi-sensei.

Okazaki-sensei once mentioned that because of his line of work, he had no time to see his girlfriend. His girlfriend, unlike the heroine of this story, had a part-time job with flexible hours. But they still had trouble making time to see each other.

On top of that, Okazaki-sensei was famous for disappearing (heh), and must have frequently stressed out his editors. The same could be said about how his girlfriend probably felt.

Because Okazaki-sensei and I were doing projects for the same magazine at the time, we had many opportunities to talk on the phone. Every so often, he would complain about how lonely he felt because he never got a chance to see his girlfriend.

WATASHI NO SUKINAHITO

わ た し の す き な ひ と

CLAMP has always been impressed by Okazaki-sensei's kindness toward women. He's the kind of guy who buys each of us a book whenever we go to the bookstore. But even an honest and kind soul like Okazaki-sensei gets stopped in his tracks when his girlfriend asks him, "Don't you want to see me?"

Girls are very complex.

It's natural to want to be with someone you love, even if it's just a crush. A girl feels both secure and content when she's with the person she loves—if only for a moment. Of course, it's also natural for lovers to experience paranoia and curiosity, but that's a whole other story.

WATASHI NO SUKINAHITO
わたしのすきなひと

TWO MONTHS AGO I WENT THROUGH A BREAKUP.
IT WAS BECAUSE OF OUR AGE DIFFERENCE.
SCENE4 A Younger Man
MY FAMILY RUNS A BAKERY, SO I'M ALWAYS BUSY.
WHAT I MEAN IS THAT I WORK IN AN OFFICE, BUT WHEN THE BAKERY IS SHORT OF HELP, I END UP HELPING OUT.
Me, working
Er, one too many.
OUR BAKERY IS ALWAYS BUSY, BUT SINCE WE MAKE CAKES HERE, AROUND CHRISTMAS SEASON...
...IT GETS ONE HUNDRED TIMES BUSIER.

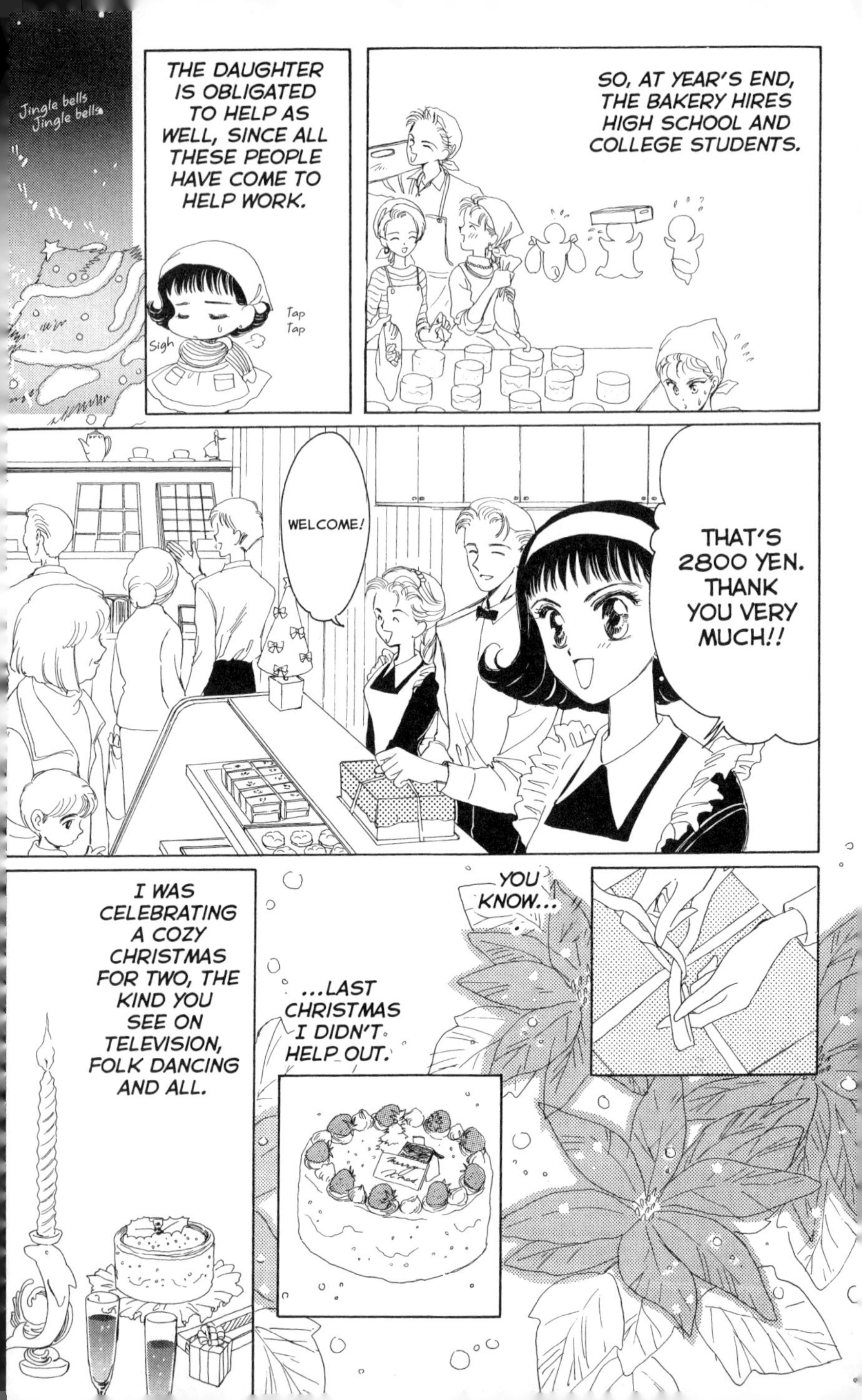
Jingle bells Jingle bells
THE DAUGHTER IS OBLIGATED TO HELP AS WELL, SINCE ALL THESE PEOPLE HAVE COME TO HELP WORK.
Tap Tap
Sigh
SO, AT YEAR'S END, THE BAKERY HIRES HIGH SCHOOL AND COLLEGE STUDENTS.
WELCOME!
THAT'S 2800 YEN. THANK YOU VERY MUCH!!
I WAS CELEBRATING A COZY CHRISTMAS FOR TWO, THE KIND YOU SEE ON TELEVISION, FOLK DANCING AND ALL.
YOU KNOW...
...LAST CHRISTMAS I DIDN'T HELP OUT.

ding-dong, ding-dong!
キーンコーンキーンコーン
ぴくぴく
YAY!
IT'S TEN O'CLOCK!!
HEY EVERYBODY, IT'S TEN! QUITTING TIME!! QUITTING TIME!!
YAY!
ガヤガヤ
GOOD WORK!
パタパタ
Let's get something to eat.
GOOD WORK, GUYS!
CHRISTMAS.
ALL THESE CAKES AND NONE FOR ME.
LAST YEAR, I BAKED MY OWN AND GAVE IT TO MY BOYFRIEND.
BUT THIS YEAR, I'LL BE SPENDING CHRISTMAS WITH "THE GUYS."
UM...
YES?
THIS BOY'S ONE OF THE PART-TIME HELPERS.
WHAT IS IT?

UH, WELL... A CAKE...
CAKE?
MAY I BUY ONE?
HUH? OH SURE, SURE.
TAKE ONE HOME. ARE YOU GOING TO EAT IT WITH YOUR FAMILY?
OR MAYBE A GIRLFRIEND?
NO...I'D RATHER BUY IT.
REALLY, IT'S OKAY.
YOU ALL HAVE WORKED SO HARD...
PLEASE LET ME PAY FOR IT.
OH, OKAY.
ALL RIGHT.
IF I REMEMBER CORRECTLY...
...HIS NEW GIRLFRIEND IS ABOUT HIS AGE.
I THINK HE MENTIONED THAT SHE WAS A SOPHOMORE IN HIGH SCHOOL.
IT'S NOT HER FAULT.

I CANNOT FORGIVE THAT JERK!!
TAKE CARE!
MERRY CHRISTMAS!
SO, HIS NEW GIRLFRIEND IS ABOUT HIS AGE.
HE WAS SELF-CONSCIOUS BECAUSE I WAS THREE YEARS OLDER THAN HIM.
AND THE LAST TIME I SAW HIM, HE BLUBBERED ON ABOUT HOW HE COULDN'T DATE AN OLDER WOMAN.
IT'S NOT LIKE I WASN'T SELF-CONSCIOUS, EITHER.
MY FRIENDS KEPT TELLING ME THAT DATING A YOUNGER GUY WAS TROUBLE.
THAT I COULD NEVER COMPETE AGAINST A YOUNGER GIRL.
I WOULD HAVE RATHER DATED SOMEONE MY OWN AGE.
BUT I DIDN'T FALL IN LOVE WITH AN AGE. IT JUST HAPPENED THAT THE BOY I FELL IN LOVE WITH WAS YOUNGER THAN ME.
WHOA!
HEY, YOU SURPRISED ME! WHAT IS IT?
DID YOU FORGET SOMETHING?

WOULD YOU...GO OUT WITH ME?
W-WHAT?!
YOU'RE TURNING SEVENTEEN THIS YEAR, RIGHT?! I'M TWENTY-FOUR!! SHOULDN'T GUYS DATE SOME CUTE GIRL THEIR AGE?!
DOES MY AGE BOTHER YOU?
WELL, WHAT ABOUT YOU...
YES, I WISH I WAS CLOSER IN AGE TO YOU, BUT...
IT'S NOT LIKE I FELL IN LOVE WITH YOU BECAUSE OF YOUR AGE.
THAT'S TRUE.
IT JUST SO HAPPENS THAT THE PERSON YOU FELL IN LOVE WITH WAS OLDER THAN YOU.

?
TODAY'S CHRISTMAS... AND I WANTED TO GIVE YOU THE MOST DELICIOUS CAKE I COULD FIND...
BUT IT'S YOUR BAKERY THAT MAKES THE BEST CAKES...
...THANK YOU.
UM, IF YOU DON'T WANT TO, THEN...
NO, I JUST REALIZED GIRLS AREN'T THE ONLY ONES HUNG UP ON AGE.
LET'S EAT THIS CAKE TOGETHER.
WHILE I POUR SOME TEA, TELL ME ABOUT YOURSELF.
SOMETHING OTHER THAN YOUR AGE.
END

SCENE·4/TOSHISHITA

(A Younger Man) としした

It seems age is always a barrier in relationships. When I was little, I loved riding on roller coasters and I always gave my parents a hard time at the amusement park because I would insist on riding them—or else. But I was only four, and the roller coasters always had height limits: "If you are shorter than this height, then you can't ride."

And, of course, I was always a lot shorter. I was also a lot younger than the six-year-old age limit. So I cried and cried, and threatened to scream and shout until they would let me on. I sang "Ookina Kuri No Shita De" (Underneath the Chestnut Tree) and danced and gave the park attendants a hard time.

I never got my wish. I began to believe that the reason I couldn't ride roller coasters was because they hated me. So I decided to hate them back and refused to ride them, even if they came up to me and apologized. I bore a total grudge against roller coasters. Ever since then, I haven't been able to ride roller coasters (although now it's because I'm scared!).

WATASHI NO SUKINAHITO

わたしのすきなひと

This story evolved from a conversation I had with the actor in the lead role of the live action version of *Tokyo Babylon,* Tonesaku Toshihide-san. In Shibuya, a few days after the last video shoot, we held a wrap party for the staff. The conversation took place on our way to sing karaoke. I don't remember what started it, but we got to talking about age and love. The guys' opinions ranged everywhere from younger girls were best, to the same age was best—all the way to—age doesn't matter. It was out of control.

The girls all laughed, "That's a guy for ya." When I asked Tonesaku-san what he thought, he chuckled and asked, "Well, what do girls think? Do they have a hang-up about age?"

"I suppose at least a little," I said "if the guy is younger, the girl gets self-conscious about being older."

"Guys feel self conscious too if they're younger." He answered with a smile.

WATASHI NO SUKINAHITO

わたしのすきなひと

They say that when you're surprised, fish scales pop out of your eyes. That being said, I would say a whole fish popped out of my eyes. (I'm not joking!) I have five girlfriends who had difficulties while dating younger guys. They all said the same thing: that while it was fun to be the older woman, they still felt insecure. For that reason, I've always assumed that women who date younger men tend to struggle in their relationships. Now, I realize that it's not just the women who feel self-conscious about it, but the men as well.

I guess age has always been a mighty wall to scale.

And with love, that wall is especially high. If any of you are bothered by being the older or younger person in the relationship, don't hold in your feelings. Just tell your partner how you feel. Chances are, they are worried and feeling insecure about something, too.

Like in my roller coaster example, a tiny seed of doubt might develop into a misunderstanding, which can then form a wall between you and the person you love.

P.S. I'd say the deterioration in my relationship with roller coasters is one hundred percent my fault.

WATASHI NO SUKINAHITO
わたしのすきなひと

WATASHI NO SUKINAHITO

わたしのすきなひと

SCENE5 SUDDENLY
AT FIRST I DIDN'T FEEL ANYTHING.
I FALL IN LOVE EASILY, BUT ALWAYS WITH GUYS WHO ARE VERY DIFFERENT FROM ME.
AT THE SAME TIME I WAS DATING A GUY, I BECAME ATTRACTED TO SOMEONE AT WORK.
LOVE ALWAYS HAPPENS SUD-DENLY.
ザワザワ
プルルルル
プルルルル
The samples are ready!
TAKE THESE COLOR PROOFS BACK TO THE PRINTER **NOW!**
OH, CAN YOU ORDER THIS 135 KG* WEIGHT PAPER FROM THE PAPER COMPANY?
*135 kg=297.62 lbs...

I WORK IN A DESIGN STUDIO.
Huh?
カサカサ
pen
バサ
バサ
OUR OFFICE DOES EVERYTHING FROM CD JACKETS TO MAGAZINES TO DIRECT MAIL, JUST ABOUT ANYTHING THAT CAN BE PRINTED.
わたわた
Huh? Huh?
ガサ
ゴソ
AGHH! WHERE'S THE CORRECTION PEN! I CAN'T FIND THE PEN!!
I HAVE TO DESIGN A CD COVER AND COLOR PROOF A PROMOTIONAL POSTER ON THE SAME DAY!
I'M A LITTLE PANICKED.
Wahhhhh! I can't find it!!
ス
UH... THANK YOU VERY MUCH.
HE'S MY BOSS, THE HEAD OF THE DESIGN TEAM.

HE'S VERY QUIET AND NOT VERY PERSONABLE, AND I CAN NEVER FIGURE OUT WHAT HE'S THINKING. IT'S LIKE HE LEFT HIS PERSONALITY A HUNDRED MILES OUTSIDE OF THE OFFICE.
FRANKLY, I DON'T REALLY GET ALONG WITH HIM.
AH! FINALLY, THE FRUITS OF OUR LABOR! I ALWAYS GET A SENSE OF ACCOMPLISHMENT WHEN THE PRODUCTS COME IN!
すりり
Mm-hmm.
OH GOODY! THEY'RE FINALLY DONE!
THE SAMPLES ARE HERE!
HE DOESN'T LOOK RIGHT, EITHER. I LIKE GUYS TO BE MORE...
Hey, let me see!
パタン
UNSOCIABLE, AS ALWAYS. CAN'T HE EVER SMILE WHEN HE SEES YOU OR GIVE HIS EMPLOYEES A PAT ON THE SHOULDER OR SOMETHING?
EH, WHO CARES? THE SAMPLES ARE HERE, AND I'M IN A GOOD MOOD.
すり

Tee hee...
SHATLAND SHEEP DOG
SHET... S...H...
?
THE TITLE IS MISSPELLED!!!
ザワ
ザワ ザワ
What? Oh, no!
buzz buzz buzz
ガターン
バサバサ

IT'S...
WRONG.
ペターン
へたへた
THE CD TITLE...OF ALL THINGS, THE CD TITLE...
AFTER WE CHECKED IT OVER AND OVER, FROM THE COPYEDIT TO THE BLUELINE TO THE COLOR PROOF.
I CHECKED EVERYTHING SO MANY TIMES...
ザワ
UM... WHERE ARE YOU GOING?
がたん
I HAVE TO APOLOGIZE TO THE CLIENT.
THAT'S RIGHT. THE SAMPLES ARE HERE.
BUT THE SAMPLES ARE ALREADY HERE.
SO I HAVE TO BITE THE BULLET AND APOLO-GIZE.
WAIT.
WE'RE DOING IT OVER.

WHAT?
THE MISTAKE IS ONLY ON THE FRONT CD COVER, RIGHT?
WHAT?
IS THIS THE ONLY MISTAKE?
I... HAVEN'T CHECKED EVERYTHING ELSE YET.
IF IT'S ONLY IN ONE PLACE, THEN WE CAN ASK THE PRINTER TO PRINT THAT PAGE OVER.
GET IN CONTACT WITH THE PRINTER IMMEDIATELY.
BUT WE DON'T HAVE ANY TIME.
I KNOW THAT.
BEING HONEST AND APOLOGIZING IS ONE WAY TO TAKE RESPONSIBILITY.
BUT, AS PROFESSIONALS, WE HAVE TO DO WHATEVER WE CAN.

I'LL GO TO THE CLIENT.
YOU CALL THE PRINTER!
THAT'S WHEN I REALIZED...
I'D FALLEN IN LOVE WITH HIM.
LOVE...
...CAN REALLY HAPPEN ALL OF A SUDDEN, CAN'T IT?
YES SIR!!
END

SCENE・5/TOTSUZEN

(Suddenly) と つ ぜ ん

Love always happens suddenly. I love a lot of things. I love Egg McMuffins from McDonalds, the plain hot dog from Mos Burger, the "Shin Megami Tensei" game from Super Famicon; Aloefan body shampoo from House of Rose, and the manga *Jojo's Strange Adventure* (especially the third generation).

I love all those things—and when I think about it—love always happens suddenly with me (just like in old-school manga). A light switches in my head, and all of a sudden, I'm in love. This story evolved from a phone conversation that I had with my trusty "brother" (heh), the manga-ka Hagiwara Kazushi-sensei. As you readers know, Hagiwara-san is the creator of *Bastard!* for *Extended Edition Jump* magazine and I've often called him prior to his frequent deadlines.

Whenever I ask him, "How are you doing?" he always answers, "I'm not doing too good physically, but I've finished the dialogue, and I've already begun rough drafts."

The four of us at CLAMP tend to worry that he pushes himself too hard. We often think Hagiwara-san puts his work before his health. We know he really loves manga and takes pride in his work (and we're proud of that), but we're also a little worried. And so, a few days later, we talked to Hagiwara-san about something else.

"So how is your manuscript coming along?" I asked.
"I'm doing the dialogue right now," he answered.
"What?! I thought you just finished the dialogue and were working on the drafts," I said with surprise.
"Oh, I'm re-doing the dialogue," Hagiwara-san replied matter-of-factly.
"B-but what about your deadline? If you're doing the dialogue now, how are you getting any sleep?"

Now, I was clearly concerned.

But Hagiwara-san went on cheerfully. "If I'm doing something for my readers, I want it to be as much fun for them as I can make it, don't you think?"

WATASHI NO SUKINAHITO
わたしのすきなひと

At that moment, I thought Hagiwara-san was really amazing. I was always his fan, but right then I fell in "love" with the artist Hagiwara Kazushi-san.

Love really can happen all of a sudden.

All of you probably have a number of reasons for falling in love. There are times when you fall in love with someone who you never thought much of before, and then there are times when someone who's been on your mind suddenly becomes the one you love.

It doesn't matter what triggers it. It doesn't have to be dramatic or cool. Whenever that "love" light bulb goes off in your heart, treasure it. It could be the first step toward a wonderful romance.

SCENE6 together
IT'S NATURAL TO WANT TO DO SOMETHING WITH THE ONE YOU LOVE.
ALL GIRLS KNOW THAT. THEY WANT TO DEVELOP SOMETHING THEY CAN SHARE WITH THE ONE THEY LOVE.
Kindergarten
ザワザワ
Hee hee!
チリリン
ザヤザヤ
ザワ
ザワ
Birthd
ents
IS SOMETHING WRONG?

?
grin
grin
I DON'T HAVE...
...AN INSTRUMENT.
HUH? BUT THE TEACHER GAVE EVERYONE ONE JUST NOW...
BUT...
I DON'T HAVE ONE.
のぞきこみ
Instruments
Peek!
IT'S EMPTY...
I KNOW.
......

OKAY, WAIT HERE!
トタタ
カターン
ダン
THIS IS MINE, BUT YOU CAN USE IT!
ポン
......?
I HAVE A HARMONICA TOO. LET'S PRACTICE TOGETHER.
COME ON KIDS, TIME FOR ORCHESTRA PRACTICE!
EVERYONE GATHER ROUND!
わら わら わら わら
COME ON, THE TEACHER'S CALLING FOR US! LET'S GO!
ぎゅっ

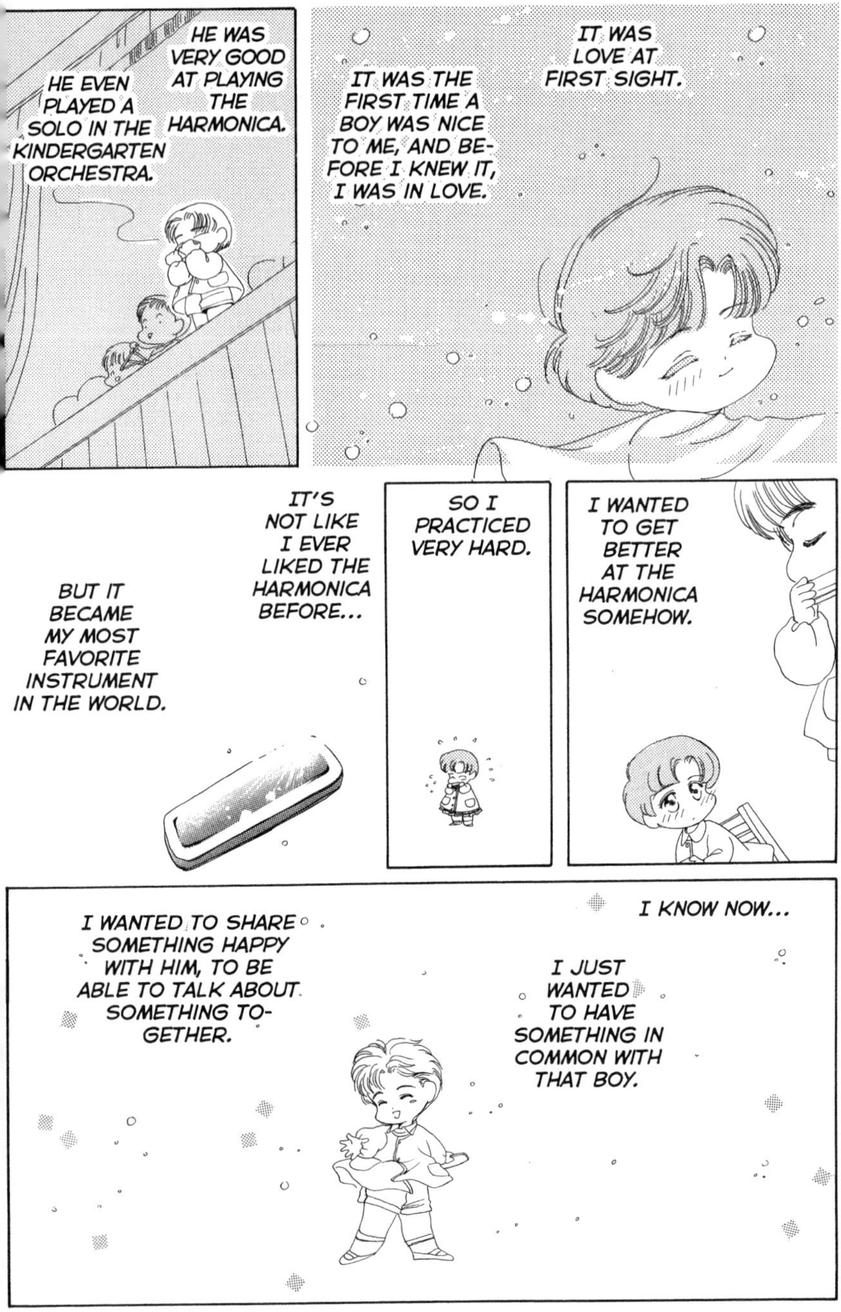
IT WAS LOVE AT FIRST SIGHT.
IT WAS THE FIRST TIME A BOY WAS NICE TO ME, AND BE-FORE I KNEW IT, I WAS IN LOVE.
HE WAS VERY GOOD AT PLAYING THE HARMONICA.
HE EVEN PLAYED A SOLO IN THE KINDERGARTEN ORCHESTRA.
I WANTED TO GET BETTER AT THE HARMONICA SOMEHOW.
SO I PRACTICED VERY HARD.
IT'S NOT LIKE I EVER LIKED THE HARMONICA BEFORE...
BUT IT BECAME MY MOST FAVORITE INSTRUMENT IN THE WORLD.
I KNOW NOW...
I JUST WANTED TO HAVE SOMETHING IN COMMON WITH THAT BOY.
I WANTED TO SHARE SOMETHING HAPPY WITH HIM, TO BE ABLE TO TALK ABOUT SOMETHING TO-GETHER.

I FELL IN LOVE WITH HIM, AND THAT'S HOW I CAME TO LOVE THE HARMONICA.
PEOPLE SAY THAT GIRLS WHO TRY TO SHARE HOBBIES OR INTERESTS WITH BOYS THEY LIKE DON'T KNOW HOW TO BE INDEPENDENT. I THINK THAT'S WRONG.
THE GIRL ISN'T TRYING TOO HARD. IT'S JUST NICE WHEN BOTH OF YOU LOVE THE SAME THING.
© SEGA
WHOA!
SORRY. I KEPT YOU WAITING BECAUSE I WAS GETTING THIS.

HERE.
BUT...YOU CAN ONLY GET THESE AT THE GAME CENTERS, RIGHT? AND I THOUGHT YOU WEREN'T GOOD AT GAMES...
BUT YOU LIKE THIS DOLL, RIGHT?
I'M STILL NOT SO HOT WITH GAMES, BUT WHEN YOU TOLD ME THAT YOU LIKED THIS DOLL, I STARTED LIKING IT TOO.
......
THANK YOU.
WHEN YOU CAN SHARE AN INTIMATE MOMENT OR A PLEASANT CONVERSATION WITH THE ONE YOU LOVE...
IT'S NEVER TRYING TOO HARD.

LET'S GO! THE MOVIE'S ABOUT TO START.
HEY.
?
DO YOU STILL LIKE THE HARMONICA?
YES.
ME TOO.

END

SCENE·6/ISSHONI

(Together) いっしょに

Being able to share your own happiness with another person is magical. I've found that when I share my happiness with someone else, my own happiness intensifies. Please don't get me wrong, not everything has to be shared. Some things are still best enjoyed while alone. But, the happiness felt when you make someone else happy, or when someone else shares in your happiness...is indescribable.

This essay is based on a story that one of CLAMP's members, Mokona Apapa-chan, told me. It takes place back in the first grade, when she fell in love with a little boy who played the harmonica. Consequently, she decided to play the harmonica, and diligently practiced every single day. I think that Mokona-chan wanted to have something in common with this boy and so became involved in what made him happy. After much practice, Mokona-chan turned into a harmonica girl who could share this hobby with her harmonica boy.

WATASHI NO SUKINAHITO

わたしのすきなひと

I've read some magazine articles that claim that girls who are influenced by their boyfriends and like the same things as them, lack both independence and their own identity, but I whole-heartedly disagree. Those girls just want to share something in common with their boyfriends. If they can learn to like the same things, then they've got something that they can do together. It's all about togetherness.

For example, if a girl starts to follow a boy's favorite soccer team, then they can go watch matches together, celebrate wins, and bemoan losses. There is no greater happiness than doing things with the one you love. And if it's something that the person you love also loves, it shouldn't be a hard thing to appreciate, right?

If you ever fall in love, you will experience the magic of sharing. And so, when you do, I hope you enjoy your time together.

WATASHI NO SUKINAHITO

わ た し の す き な ひ と

I WANT TO BE PRETTY.
ALL GIRLS DO.
ESPECIALLY WHEN THEY ARE IN LOVE.
AND SO DO I.
SCENE7 pretty
ざ———っ
パラ パラ
WHY...
WHY DOES IT HAVE TO RAIN?!

I PICKED OUT EVERYTHING YESTERDAY!
ぽい
ぽい
THE CLOTHES!
THE PURSE!
THE SHOES!
EVEN THE JEWELRY!
I TOOK TWO HOURS TO SELECT EVERYTHING!
IT WAS GOING TO BE PERFECT!
I EVEN CURLED MY HAIR BEFORE I WENT TO BED!
MY HAIR IS STRAIGHT, BUT CURLY GOES BETTER WITH THIS OUTFIT.
IT TOOK OVER AN HOUR!
AND LOOK!
WHY?! WHY DOES IT HAVE TO RAIN TODAY?!
THE SKIRT I PICKED OUT IS LONG AND WHITE. SO IF I GET DIRT ON IT I'LL CRY, FOR SURE.

WITH THE HUMIDITY..
LOOK.
MY CURLS ARE COMING OUT ALREADY!
Dun-dun!
OH, HOW COULD THIS BE HAPPENING TO ME?!
GOD, YOU'RE SO EVIL!
TODAY'S THE DAY I WANTED TO LOOK MY PRETTIEST!
OKAY...WELL I JUST WANTED TO LOOK AS PRETTY AS I COULD.
TODAY IS THE DAY I CAN BE WITH THE ONE I LOVE...
AGHHH!
A-A-ALREADY TWO O'CLOCK?!
WE'RE SUPPOSED TO MEET AT THREE! THE TRAIN TAKES THIRTY MINUTES AND I ONLY HAVE THIRTY MINUTES TO PICK OUT MY CLOTHES, DO MY MAKEUP AND GET TO THE STATION!
大パニック
Major Panic

I-I'LL JUST WEAR THIS!
ぱっ
A-AND I'LL TAKE THIS PURSE!
AND MY SHOES...!
OH NO!
BUT ONLY ONE PAIR OF SHOES WILL MATCH THIS OUTFIT!
AND I CAN'T WEAR THOSE ON A RAINY DAY!
THEN THIS!
THIS ONE-PIECE AND THIS PURSE!!
BUT I WORE THIS THE LAST TIME WE MET.
THEN THIS IS IT! THIS, THIS AND THIS!
Aghhhh!
I'm-not-giving-up!
IT...
IT DOESN'T MATCH AT ALL.
WAHHH! I CAN'T STAND THIS!
NOTHING LOOKS GOOD ON ME! IT DOESN'T MATTER WHAT I WEAR!

FORGET IT! I'LL JUST WEAR THIS!!!
I'M LATE!!!
I'D BE BETTER OFF WEARING A GODZILLA COSTUME AND TRYING TO PLAY IT OFF FOR LAUGHS!
HE'S GOING TO HATE ME! HE'S GOING TO BE SICK OF ME!
HE MIGHT'VE EVEN THOUGHT I WAS A LITTLE PRETTY.
IF IT WERE SUNNY, AT LEAST I'D LOOK BETTER THAN I DO NOW.
OH GOD... WHY COULDN'T YOU BE ON MY SIDE JUST THIS ONE DAY?
BUT NO...
TODAY I HAVE TO BE THE UGLIEST GIRL ON EARTH!

ザワ
ザワ
SORRY.
I'M LATE...
こつん
HEY, YOU'RE *THIRTY MINUTES LATE*. DID SOMETHING HAPPEN?
No. No.
I WAS WORRIED. YOU'RE ALWAYS ON TIME... BESIDES, IT WAS RAINING.

...I'M SORRY.
WELL, YOU'RE LOOKING EXTRA PRETTY TODAY, SO I FORGIVE YOU.
ぴくっ
?!
THAT OUTFIT LOOKS REALLY GREAT ON YOU.
LET'S GO, I BET YOU'RE HUNGRY.
I TAKE IT BACK, GOD.
THANK YOU FOR LETTING IT RAIN.

END

SCENE・7/KIREI

(Pretty) きれい

All girls want to be told they're pretty. Sure, some might say: "I don't want to be pretty," or "I'm pretty enough," but frankly, why wouldn't you want to be thought of as pretty?

I understand that beauty is subjective. What one person might consider beautiful, another might not. I also understand that *feeling* pretty and *being* pretty are two very different things. Some people might not think you're pretty, but if you *feel* pretty then that's all that matters.

With that being said, I'd like to share a story about something that happened to Igarashi Satsuki-chan in kindergarten. At the time, Sa-chan (as she's called by CLAMP) was a very quiet child, who was constantly bullied by all the kindergarten boys—except one—who would actually protect her.

Everyday, Sa-chan would look forward to seeing the boy. Before he came to class, she would smooth her uniform, wipe her schoolbag, and shine her shoes. And do you know why she would take such care before she saw the boy? Because she wanted to look pretty for the one she loved.

WATASHI NO SUKINAHITO
わたしのすきなひと

Whether in kindergarten or high school, married or single, most girls want to feel pretty for the ones they love. Some people actually think that women become prettier when they're in love. I'm not convinced of that just yet, but it kind of makes sense. Let's see...

In order to be in love, you must fall in love. And when you fall in love with someone, you hope that person has fallen in love with you. So it's only natural that you would want to be as pretty as possible when this person sees you, right? Maybe girls cast a spell on themselves to make their love stronger? I don't know.

But what I do know is...at least twelve girls who have fallen in love have become prettier. Out of those, nine got married and became wonderful housewives. So please remember to cast your spells, so that you, too, will be able to experience the richness of love.

WATASHI NO SUKINAHITO
わたしのすきなひと

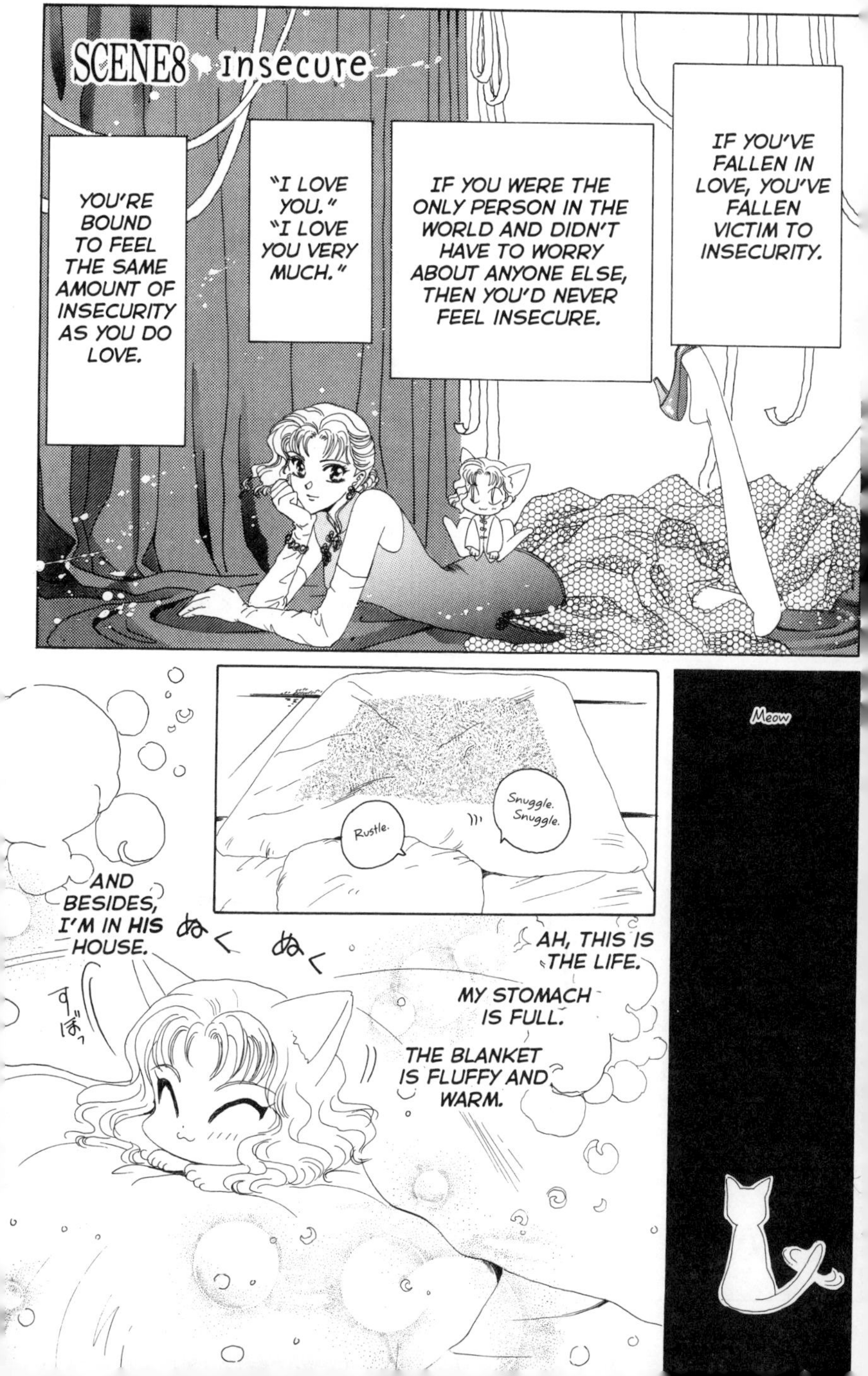

SCENE8 Insecure
IF YOU'VE FALLEN IN LOVE, YOU'VE FALLEN VICTIM TO INSECURITY.
IF YOU WERE THE ONLY PERSON IN THE WORLD AND DIDN'T HAVE TO WORRY ABOUT ANYONE ELSE, THEN YOU'D NEVER FEEL INSECURE.
"I LOVE YOU." "I LOVE YOU VERY MUCH."
YOU'RE BOUND TO FEEL THE SAME AMOUNT OF INSECURITY AS YOU DO LOVE.
Meow
Snuggle. Snuggle.
Rustle.
AH, THIS IS THE LIFE.
MY STOMACH IS FULL.
THE BLANKET IS FLUFFY AND WARM.
AND BESIDES, I'M IN HIS HOUSE.
ぬく ぬく
すぽっ

I WISH I COULD STAY HERE FOREVER.
Yawn...
I WISH I COULD BE THIS HAPPY FOREVER.
うにうに
ひょいっ
WHAT?! WHAT IS IT?!
meow
meow
WHAT
PPENED!!
I WANT TO STAY IN THIS ROOM!
I WANT TO STAY!
WHY ARE YOU BEING SO MEAN?!
ずん ずん ずん ずん ずん ずん ずん ずん
ガラ
NOOOO!! IT'S COLD!! I DON'T WANT TO GO OUTSIDE, IT'S COLD!
Brr! Brr! Brr! Brr!
ポイ

WHY?
IT'S COLD OUTSIDE! THE SNOW IS COLD! WHY WON'T YOU LET ME STAY IN YOUR ROOM?!
カラカラ
BECAUSE I DON'T NEED YOU ANYMORE!
ガーン
OPEN UP!
DON'T BE MEAN TO ME! DON'T DUMP ME!!
にゃにゃにゃにゃにゃにゃにゃ
カリカリカリカリカリカリ
OPEN THE DOOR! IT'S COLD! I'M SAD! I'M LONELY!
meow meow
scratch scratch

WHAT A BAD DREAM...
IT'S A REOCCURRING DREAM.
THE STORY CHANGES, BUT THE END NEVER DOES.
HE TELLS ME HE DOESN'T NEED ME ANYMORE.
I'M WORRIED.
I LOVE HIM, BUT MAYBE HE DOESN'T FEEL THE SAME WAY.
HE MIGHT HAVE LOVED ME YESTERDAY, BUT HE HATES ME TODAY.

I LOVE HIM, AND THAT'S WHY I FEEL INSECURE.
OPENING THE DOOR IS HARD AFTER THAT DREAM...
?
ガタ ガタ
WHAT?! THIS IS THE SPARE KEY THAT HE GAVE ME, BUT THE DOOR WON'T OPEN!
DOES THIS MEAN HE DOESN'T WANT ME AROUND ANYMORE?!
MAYBE I'M BEING DUMPED.
WAS THAT DREAM A PREMONITION?!
Meow!
It's cold!
WHAT ARE YOU DOING?
AGHHH!!
ガラッ

HURRY UP AND GET INSIDE. YOU'LL TURN INTO A SNOWMAN.
UH, UMM...MY KEY...DIDN'T WORK...
Meow?
うにゃ
ふぅ
パラパラ
Oh, thank you.
I TOLD YOU LAST WEEK THAT I CHANGED THE LOCK.
Now you tell me.

OH GOOD... THAT DREAM WASN'T A PREMONITION.
DID YOU SAY SOMETHING?
NOTHING.
LOVE IS MATCHED BY INSECURITY. FOR THE NUMBER OF DAYS YOU'RE IN LOVE, THERE'S AN EQUAL NUMBER OF DAYS YOU'RE INSECURE.
BUT WITH EACH DAY, I FALL THAT MUCH MORE IN LOVE WITH YOU.

END

SCENE·8/FUAN

(Insecure) ふあん

I think girls become insecure when they fall in love. I can't speak for boys, but it would make sense that they would feel insecure, too. In order to love someone, you have to open your heart, and when you open your heart, it can be scary. It can also be uncomfortable and exhilarating, depending on how you look at it. But, when your heart is open, you are open as well.

Everything feels different when you're in love. Of course, you still feel sorrow and pain, but for the most part—love makes you happy. The flip side to love's euphoria is the fear that the magic and butterflies will disappear (and that's no fun!).

WATASHI NO SUKINAHITO

わたしのすきなひと

I got the idea for this story from a long phone conversation I had with a friend late one night. This friend was in love with an older man, and she told me how in love and happy she was with him. But at the same time, she wondered how long her happiness would last. It seems that the happier you are, the more scared you become that your happiness might end.

I've found that predicting the ways of the heart is more difficult than predicting tomorrow's exchange rates. And so, I don't think there's any way to eliminate all the insecurity involved with love. It's simply part of the package. (Not the prettiest wrapping, I know!)

Should any of you find a way to reduce your insecurity, then please let me know because I carry the heavy burden, too.

WATASHI NO SUKINAHITO

わたしのすきなひと

FEBRUARY 14TH IS VALENTINE'S DAY.
I ALWAYS WONDERED...
HOW DID VALENTINE'S DAY COME ABOUT?
AND WHY DOES VALENTINE'S DAY MAKE US WANT TO CONFESS OUR LOVE?
SCENE9 courage
St. Valentine
St. Valentine

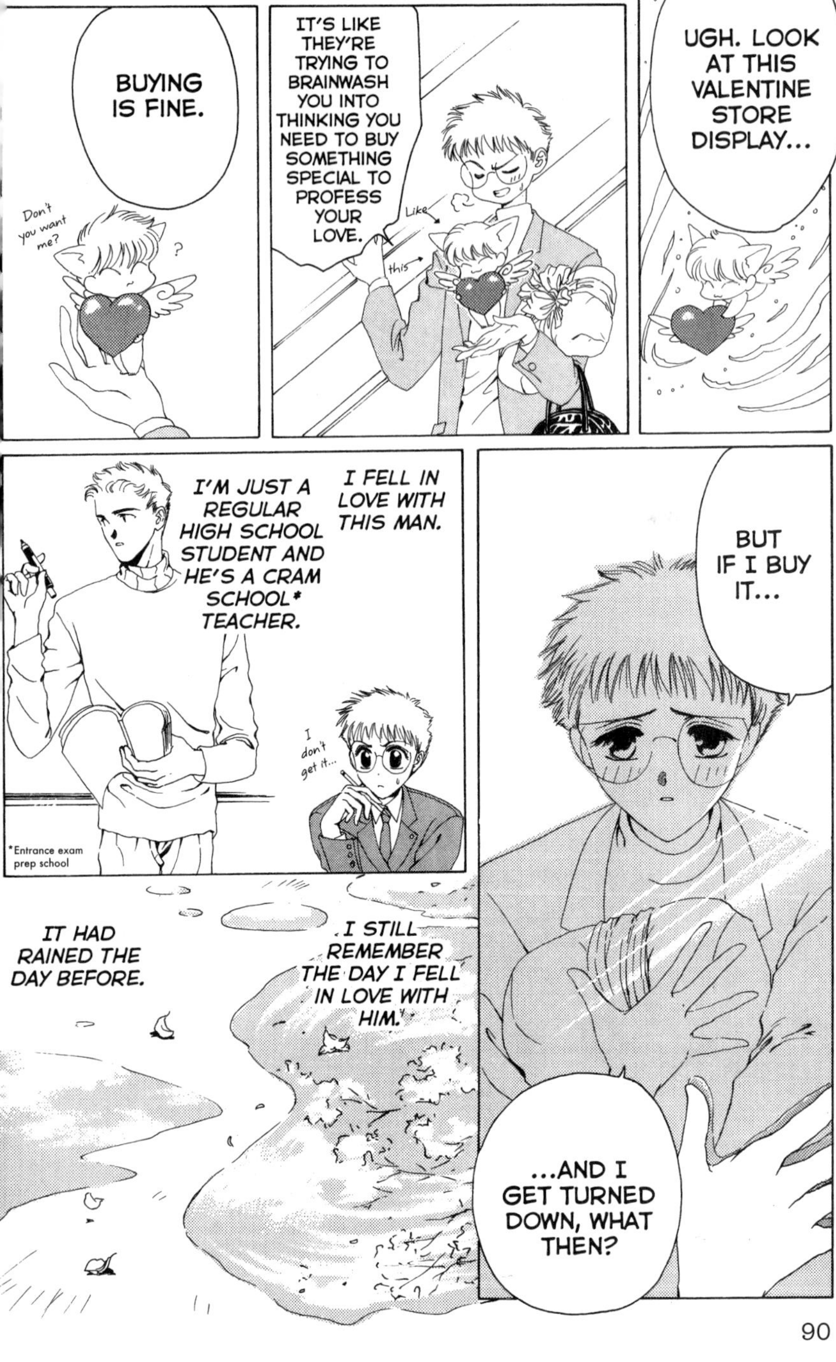
UGH. LOOK AT THIS VALENTINE STORE DISPLAY...
IT'S LIKE THEY'RE TRYING TO BRAINWASH YOU INTO THINKING YOU NEED TO BUY SOMETHING SPECIAL TO PROFESS YOUR LOVE.
Like
this
BUYING IS FINE.
Don't you want me?
?
BUT IF I BUY IT...
I FELL IN LOVE WITH THIS MAN.
I'M JUST A REGULAR HIGH SCHOOL STUDENT AND HE'S A CRAM SCHOOL* TEACHER.
I don't get it...
*Entrance exam prep school
I STILL REMEMBER THE DAY I FELL IN LOVE WITH HIM.
IT HAD RAINED THE DAY BEFORE.
...AND I GET TURNED DOWN, WHAT THEN?

Whoa, whoa! It's wet
ぱしゃ
?!
ずる
OH NOOOO! MY HAND-KNITTED SWEATER!!
ぺたん
ばたばた
ぱしゃ
ぱしゃ
Panicking
すっ
ぐいっ
EEK!
Whoa!

?
?
バサ
パサ
UGHH...IT'S A SCENE RIGHT OUT OF A GIRLS' MANGA.

I'VE ASKED HIM TO THE MOVIES SEVERAL TIMES AFTER THAT.
BUT IT'S ALWAYS ME CALLING HIM. HE NEVER CALLS ME.
I KNOW I KNOW. I'M OUT OF MY LEAGUE. I'M JUST A CRAM SCHOOL STUDENT.
TODAY IS VALENTINE'S DAY.
A DAY TO TELL YOUR TRUE FEELINGS.
I BOUGHT HIM SOME CHOCOLATES AND A SWEATER.
I'M SCARED THAT EVEN IF I TELL HIM HOW I FEEL, IT WON'T DO ANY GOOD.
IF IT HADN'T BEEN VALENTINE'S DAY...
...I MIGHT NOT HAVE HAD THE COURAGE...
...TO TELL HIM HOW I FELT.
I LOVE YOU!
?!
ずいっ

UH...
YOU PROBABLY DON'T WANT TO BE BOTHERED WITH SOMETHING LIKE THIS...
...BUT I'M IN LOVE WITH YOU.
UM...
UM...
UM...
Heh.
THANK YOU.
WHAAAAT?! R-REALLY REALLY?!
REALLY WHAT?
UH...

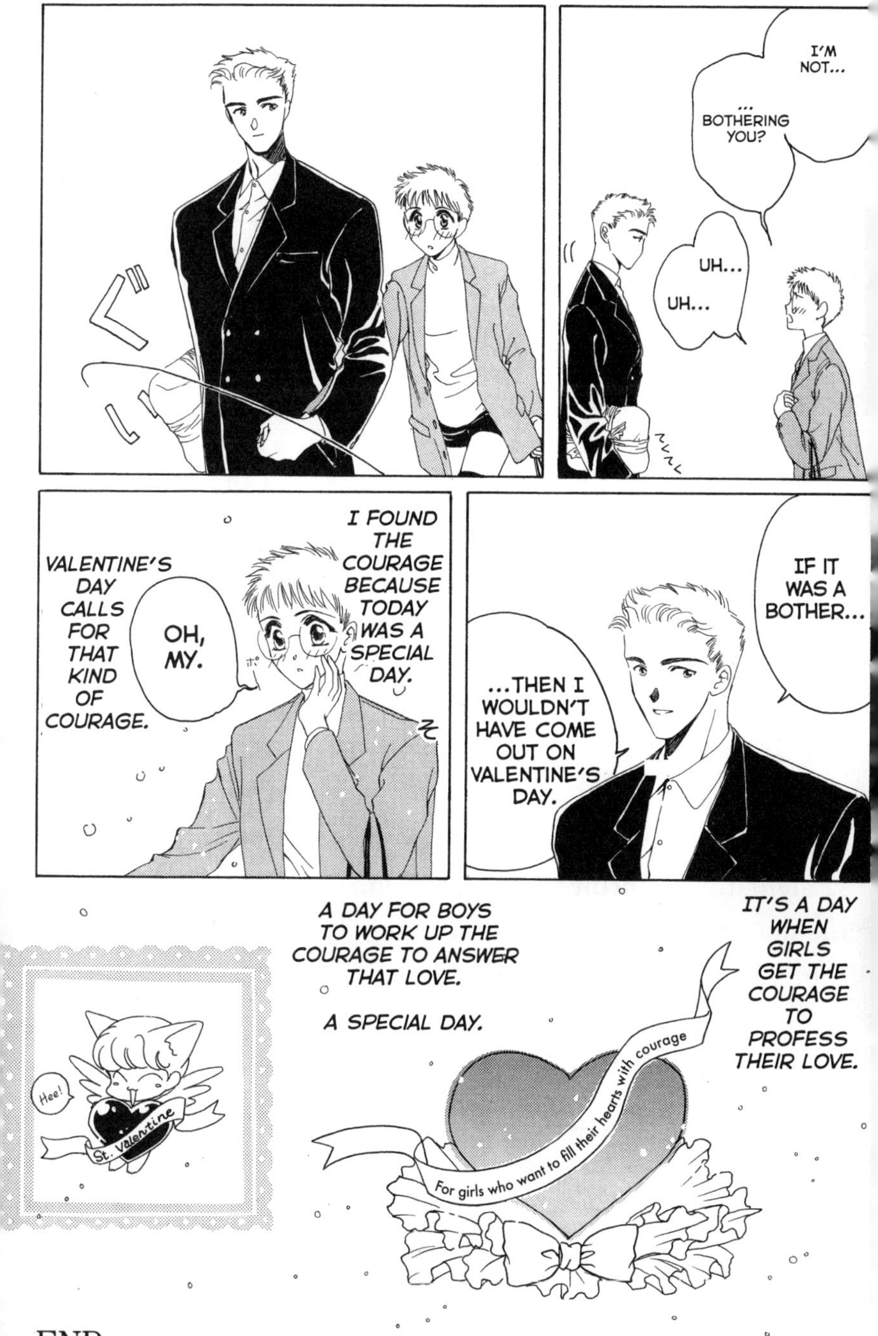
UH...
UH...
I'M NOT...
...BOTHERING YOU?
OH, MY.
VALENTINE'S DAY CALLS FOR THAT KIND OF COURAGE.
I FOUND THE COURAGE BECAUSE TODAY WAS A SPECIAL DAY.
IF IT WAS A BOTHER...
...THEN I WOULDN'T HAVE COME OUT ON VALENTINE'S DAY.
IT'S A DAY WHEN GIRLS GET THE COURAGE TO PROFESS THEIR LOVE.
A DAY FOR BOYS TO WORK UP THE COURAGE TO ANSWER THAT LOVE.
A SPECIAL DAY.
For girls who want to fill their hearts with courage
Hee!
St. Valentine

END

SCENE·9/YÛKI

(Courage) ゆうき

I wanted to do a story about Valentine's Day, because we at CLAMP love special occasions. And Valentine's Day definitely qualifies as a special occasion. On Christmas, we get cakes. On Halloween, we watch horror movies on video (ok, maybe not). Anyway, we just love our events.

Just so you know, this story first appeared in the February issue of the magazine *Young Rose*. February is all about Valentine's Day. And Valentine's Day is all about beans! Actually, for a moment, I thought writing a bean story would be cool, but instead I decided on a Valentine's Day story, since I love chocolate so much. (Don't worry, I love beans too!)

We at CLAMP have had only a few opportunities to do a straight-up Valentine's Day story. One reason was because the magazine that publishes us doesn't run "seasonal" things.

And, the other reason was because we've never created a heroine who would say something like, "Oh, February 14th is Valentine's Day. I have to buy some chocolates and send them to that boy!" Especially in *Asuka* magazine, where the main character, Bou, is not in any position to receive any chocolates.

Anyway, back to Valentine's Day. I'm sure you all know that sending chocolates is not a universal ritual. I think the person who started the tradition of sending chocolate on Valentine's Day was the president of a candy company (I can't be sure, though).

But, regardless of the holiday's origin, Valentine's Day is still a special day for girls. February 14th is the one day we're "allowed" to tell someone how we feel.

WATASHI NO SUKINAHITO

わたしのすきなひと

I don't have any scientific evidence, but it seems that on Valentine's Day, girls have ten times the amount of courage than they normally have.

So...for those of you who have a certain someone, but are unable to express your feelings—Valentine's Day just might turbocharge your engine!

MARRIAGE IS CHALLENGING.
HOW DO ALL THOSE COUPLES CROSS THE THRESHOLD FROM "LOVE" INTO MARRIAGE"?
WHAT LIFE-ALTERING EVENT CONVINCES THEM TO MARRY?
SCENE10 Normal

ピー
ポリ
は
W-WHOOAA!!
わたた
UGH. I HAVE A BAD HABIT OF LETTING MY HANDS GO IDLE WHEN I GET LOST IN THOUGHT.
Phew...
THE CURRY'S SAFE.
Blub
Blub
I WONDER HOW MANY TIMES I'VE COOKED FOR HIM.
THE FIRST TIME WE MET WAS AT OUR COMPANY'S CHERRY BLOSSOM VIEWING PARTY.
WE'D NEVER SPOKE BEFORE, BEING IN DIFFERENT DIVISIONS.

BUT MY FIRST IMPRESSION OF HIM WAS THAT HE WAS STRANGE.
AFTERWARD, I HEARD THAT HE LOVED CHERRY BLOSSOMS AND HAD BEEN TOO EXCITED TO CONTAIN HIMSELF.
THAT DAY, I'D MADE BENTO.
Munch Munch
Hey, don't hog it all! Lemme have some...
Munch
Munch
MY FAMILY RUNS A RESTAURANT. I GUESS THAT'S WHY I'VE LOVED TO COOK SINCE I WAS SMALL.
Scoop out the inside of the tomato. Stuff it with onions, tuna and mayo.
Potato Salad—Large Portions

YOU'RE AN EXCELLENT COOK.
AFTER THAT, WE STARTED DATING. IT'S BEEN TWO YEARS NOW.
ON MY LAST BIRTHDAY, HE SAID "LET'S GET MARRIED."
BUT SINCE WE STARTED DATING SO NONCHALANTLY...
...I DON'T KNOW HOW TO MAKE THE JUMP FROM LOVE...
...TO MARRIAGE.

ding-dong
COMING!
パタパタ
SOMETHING SMELLS GOOD!
I MADE CURRY TODAY.
Yay!
HE'S A GOOD PERSON, AND I LOVE HIM.
BUT I DON'T KNOW IF...
...WHAT I'M FEELING CAN TURN INTO MARRIAGE.

I'm going to try the salad.
SECONDS, PLEASE!
What's up? You're smiling.
Great salad.
WHAT AN APPETITE.
You ate two helpings of tomato salad.
WHEN YOU EAT SO HEARTILY, IT MAKES ME...
...WANT TO COOK FOR YOU ALWAYS.
UH, WHAT IS IT?
IS SOME-THING WRONG?
Did you want that tomato?

NO.
THAT'S NOT IT.
I SEE. IT'S SIMPLE.
THAT'S NOT IT.
TO GET MARRIED...
?
...YOU DON'T NEED ANYTHING SPECIAL.
I JUST WANT TO BE WITH YOU ALL THE TIME, AND THAT'S WHAT MATTERS.
I WANT TO COOK FOR YOU ALWAYS.
IF CHERISHING EVERYDAY FEELINGS IS ALL WE NEED, WE'LL MAKE A WONDERFUL COUPLE.
?
LET'S GET MARRIED.
END

SCENE・10/FUTSÛ

(Normal) ふつう

Hey readers, are you married yet? None of us at CLAMP is married. But, like most girls of marrying age, (how much longer do we have, anyways?) we all aspire to become brides.

I thought up this story when three of my friends got married, one after the other. Even though the women varied in age, occupation, and birthplace; they all shared one thing, which managed to leave a lasting impression on me. Each woman said they got married because they thought they'd have a "normal life" with their husbands.

None of the brides seemed to think that what they had said was significant, but I found it very interesting. Since I'm single, marriage is uncharted territory.

WATASHI NO SUKINAHITO

わたしのすきなひと

Because I'm not married (and never have been), I have no idea what it's like to be a wife. I'm also not clued in to a husband's trials and tribulations. I have always thought marriage was a special thing that required a huge amount of resolve. So, when my three friends said that the reason they got married was because they thought they could live normal lives, I found it very surprising.

Then I realized something. I suppose the idea of two strangers becoming a couple could seem like a bizarre ritual. But, the "formality" of marriage only lasts a moment, and then, the couple goes back to their normal everyday life. The sun comes up again, just as it did before they got married. They wake up, eat breakfast, and go to work—just like the day before.

WATASHI NO SUKINAHITO

わたしのすきなひと

Now, I understand that those three couples chose partners who they thought they could share a normal life with.

I'm afraid, however, it might be awhile before I get to experience either normalcy or marriage (ha ha).

I WONDER WHO SAID THAT LOVE AND DISTANCE WERE PRO-PORTIONAL?
THE FARTHER THE DISTANCE BETWEEN TWO PEOPLE, THE FARTHER APART THEIR HEARTS STRAY.
I DON'T BELIEVE THAT.
BUT IT MIGHT BE EASIER IF I DID.
SCENE11 Apart
AT FIRST, WE WERE CLOSE.
Does this look good?

BY BIKE HIS HOUSE WAS ONLY THREE MINUTES AWAY
His House
My House
WE LIVED SO CLOSE TO EACH OTHER WE USED TO LAUGH AND SAY THAT WE WERE WASTING MONEY ON PHONE BILLS.
NOW...
...IT'S A TOTAL LONG DISTANCE RELATIONSHIP.
めめ
めめ
I'M NOT DOING THIS LONG DISTANCE THING BECAUSE I LIKE IT.
WE'RE STILL HIGH SCHOOL STUDENTS, AFTER ALL. AND HE HAD TO MOVE BECAUSE OF HIS FATHER'S JOB.
WE HAVE NO CONTROL OVER IT!
Chomp Chomp
WE LIVE SO FAR APART THAT I'M AFRAID TO CALL BECAUSE OF THE PHONE BILL.

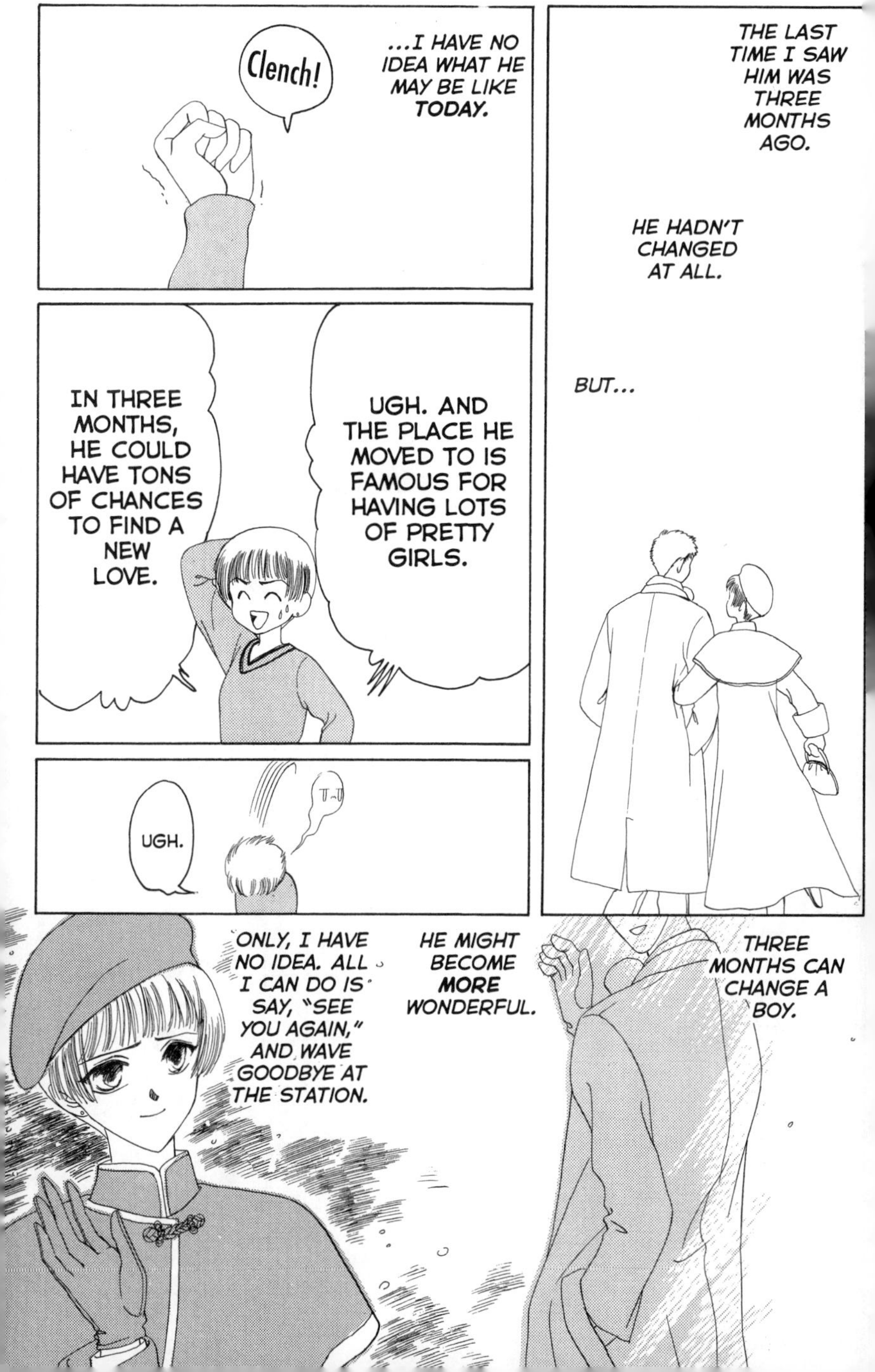

THE LAST TIME I SAW HIM WAS THREE MONTHS AGO.
HE HADN'T CHANGED AT ALL.
BUT...
...I HAVE NO IDEA WHAT HE MAY BE LIKE TODAY.
Clench!
UGH. AND THE PLACE HE MOVED TO IS FAMOUS FOR HAVING LOTS OF PRETTY GIRLS.
IN THREE MONTHS, HE COULD HAVE TONS OF CHANCES TO FIND A NEW LOVE.
UGH.
THREE MONTHS CAN CHANGE A BOY.
HE MIGHT BECOME MORE WONDERFUL.
ONLY, I HAVE NO IDEA. ALL I CAN DO IS SAY, "SEE YOU AGAIN," AND WAVE GOODBYE AT THE STATION.

IF HE FINDS SOMEONE NICE OVER THERE, I CAN'T DO ANYTHING ABOUT IT.
All right then, I'm going!
I GUESS THE HEART CAN'T OVERCOME DISTANCE.
NO MATTER HOW HARD I TRY, IT SEEMS IMPOSSIBLE.
WHEN WE'RE THIS FAR APART, WE CAN'T EVEN HOLD HANDS.

ザワ
ザワ ザワ
The next train will arrive at platform three...
FIVE MINUTES HAVE GONE BY...
I'M GETTING WORRIED...
WILL HE REALLY COME?
MAYBE HE'S FORGOTTEN ABOUT ME...
...AND THE PROMISE WE HAD MADE THREE MONTHS AGO. MAYBE HE'S ALREADY OFF WALKING ARM-IN-ARM WITH SOME GIRL...
AH! I'M GETTING DEPRESSED.
Rrruuummmmble...

?!
W-WHAT HAPPENED? WHY WERE YOU RUNNING SO HARD?
ACCIDENT... TRAIN... DELAYED...
AND I WAS MAKING YOU WAIT ...
... SO I RAN ...
...AT TOP SPEED...
HEY.
?

DID YOU WANT TO SEE ME?
IF I DIDN'T, I WOULDN'T HAVE SAVED UP MONEY FOR THIS TICKET, OR HAVE BEEN IN SUCH A RUSH.
YEAH, RIGHT.
SO THAT'S IT.
IT'S NOT DISTANCE THAT RUINS A RELATIONSHIP.
AS LONG AS YOU WANT TO SEE EACH OTHER, LOVE CAN LAST.
YOUR HEART DOESN'T GROW DISTANT BECAUSE YOU'RE APART.
IF YOUR HEART GROWS DISTANT, IT MIGHT BE FOR OTHER REASONS.
AS LONG AS YOU WANT TO SEE EACH OTHER, YOUR HEARTS WILL BE CLOSE TOGETHER.
WHAT ARE YOU SMILING ABOUT?
NOTHING. I JUST WANTED TO SEE YOU TOO.
END

SCENE·11/HANARERU
(Apart) はなれる

Long distance relationships are challenging. The longest long-distance couple that I know is an Osaka-Norway pair. But, it doesn't have to be a trans-continental relationship for it to be considered long distance. Regardless of actual distance, when you can't see each other—it's hard.

This story is about my friend, a magazine editor, who told me about the time she professed her love to someone. All jobs are hard, but my friend was assigned to an extremely demanding division of a weekly magazine. For this job, she had to move from Osaka to Tokyo, and consequently, left her college boyfriend back in Osaka.

Osaka and Tokyo are about three hours apart by shinkansen (bullet train). Some people might be insulted if I said this was far, but still, it's not the kind of distance where you could casually plan an impromptu date.

WATASHI NO SUKINAHITO

わたしのすきなひと

On top of that, she's a magazine editor, so even if a date is planned on such-and-such day or such-and-such month, there's no telling whether or not writers will deliver their manuscripts on time.

Consequently, many dates were canceled, even though the boyfriend had cleared his busy schedule. Somehow, my friend has been able to sustain this Osaka-Tokyo long distance relationship.

When I see how many people fail at long distance relationships, I admire how my friend was able to continue moving forward with hers, even though they frequently quarreled. When I told her how I felt, she said: "Even though it might be a long distance relationship, in our hearts, we aren't far apart."

Ahh, so true. Despite the distance, there are lots of ways couples can communicate—by phone, by mail, by internet. As long as your hearts are together, your love will not die. There's some psychology for you!

P.S. Soon my friend will convert her long distance relationship into a long distance marriage!

WATASHI NO SUKINAHITO

わたしのすきなひと

I'M GOING TO BE MARRIED.
AND I'M ALL NERVES.
SCENE12 Marriage
ザワザワ
パタパタ

I'M ABOUT TO BE MARRIED.
TODAY IS THE DAY.
Sigh...
ぱたん
ぱたぱた
ARE YOU READY?!
Oh my! As they say, "the clothes make the horse!" How pretty!
I think you mean, "the clothes make the man."
ARE YOU HUNGRY? HERE, HAVE A SANDWICH!
I'm jealous. I wish I could wear one too.
YOU SHOULD EAT NOW!
AS YOU KNOW, THE BRIDE IS FORBIDDEN TO ENJOY THE BIG FEAST LATER.
SIS, I SAW YOU EATING WHILE YOU WERE CHANGING OUT OF YOUR KIMONO AND INTO YOUR WEDDING DRESS.
Ho ho ho!
What an appetite!

HO HO HO! SHE HASN'T EATEN ALL MORNING 'CAUSE SHE'S BEEN SO NERVOUS! SHE MUST HAVE FINALLY GONE NUTS.
WHAT'S WRONG?
DO YOU HAVE A STOMACH-ACHE?
Oh, my.
IT'S NOTHING.
I JUST COULDN'T SLEEP LAST NIGHT.
ふるる
YOU? THE SISTER WITH THE MOST POISE?
WHO NEVER HAS A CARE IN THE WORLD?
EVEN I CAN GET NERVES...
...ON THE DAY OF MY WEDDING!!
WILL THE FAMILY OF THE BRIDE PLEASE ENTER!
WE NEED TO GO, SO MAKE SURE YOU EAT.
COMING!

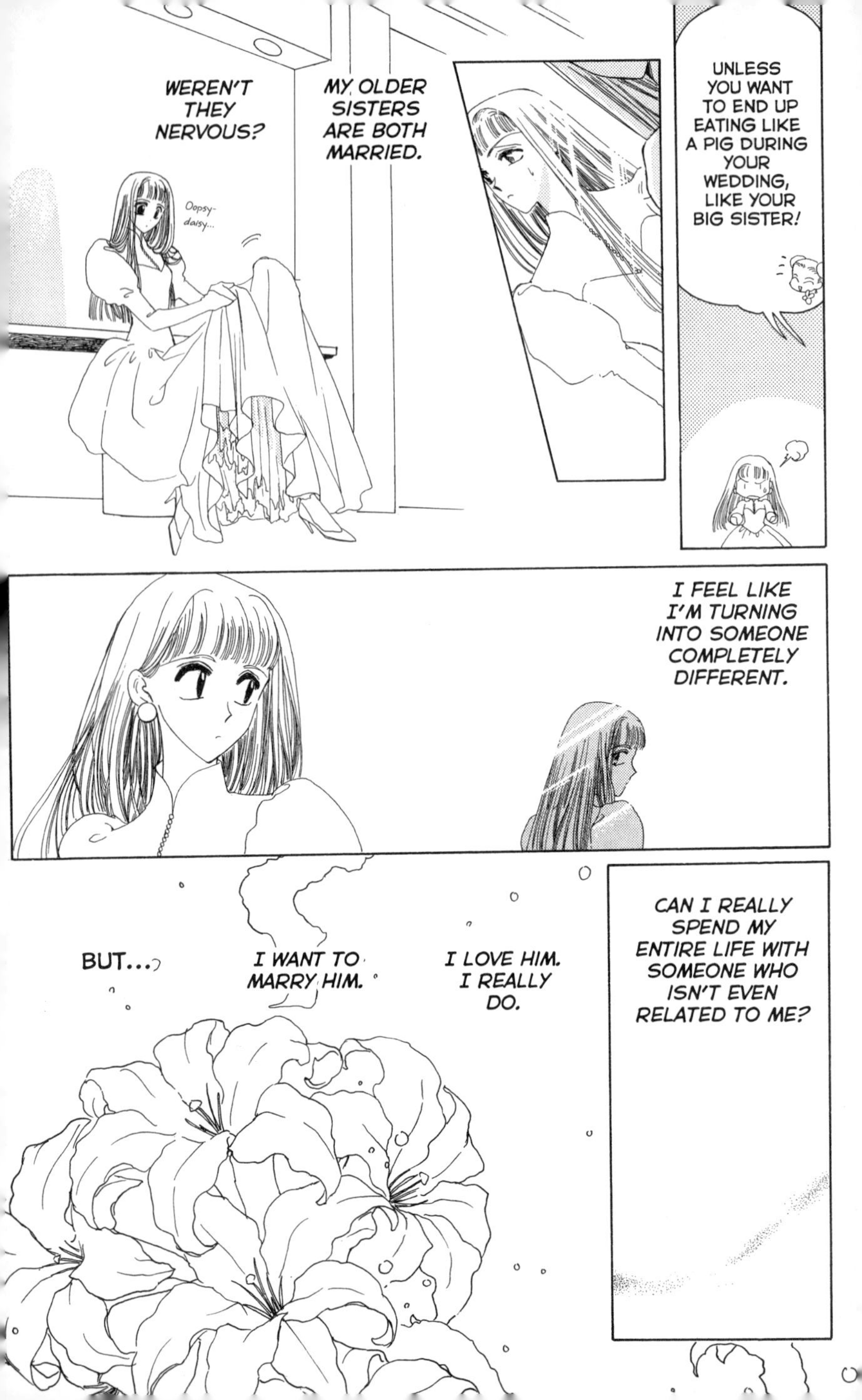
UNLESS YOU WANT TO END UP EATING LIKE A PIG DURING YOUR WEDDING, LIKE YOUR BIG SISTER!
MY OLDER SISTERS ARE BOTH MARRIED.
WEREN'T THEY NERVOUS?
Oopsy-daisy...
I FEEL LIKE I'M TURNING INTO SOMEONE COMPLETELY DIFFERENT.
CAN I REALLY SPEND MY ENTIRE LIFE WITH SOMEONE WHO ISN'T EVEN RELATED TO ME?
I LOVE HIM. I REALLY DO.
I WANT TO MARRY HIM.
BUT...

I'M AFRAID I MIGHT CHANGE ONCE I'M MARRIED.
MAYBE I'M RUSHING INTO THIS.
THINGS MIGHT NOT GO AS PLANNED ONCE WE'RE MARRIED.
MAYBE HE'LL FIND HE LIKED ME BETTER BEFORE WE WERE MARRIED.
IF WE GET INTO A FIGHT, BREAKING UP IS NOT AS SIMPLE.
VISION OF PROPERTY
ALIMONY PAYMENTS
DIVORCE PAPERS
PARENTAL RIGHTS
Sob Sob
WAAAAAH!

I!
I!!
Ka-dun
WOW. WHAT A PRETTY BRIDE.
I! I! I!
I MIGHT CHANGE ONCE I'M MARRIED!
WHAT'S WRONG WITH THAT?
WHEN WE GET MARRIED, I MIGHT BECOME A DIFFERENT PERSON!
HUH?

BEFORE, WE DID THINGS THAT SINGLE PEOPLE DO. AND WHEN WE GET MARRIED, WE'LL DO THINGS THAT ONLY A MARRIED COUPLE CAN DO.
SO FOR NOW, WHY DON'T WE CONCENTRATE ON DOING MARRIED-COUPLE THINGS.
OKAY?
OKAY!
END

SCENE·12/KEKKON

(Marriage) けっこん

Although my older sister and I are eight years apart, she would always come to me for advice about everything from work, friends, and of course—love. When my sister was little, she knew that she wanted to be a kindergarten teacher when she grew up (which she eventually did become).

My sister was one of those happy-go-lucky types, who was always grounded and level headed. Sure, sometimes she felt anxious, but it never hindered her judgment or drive. Except when it came to the boy she was dating, and whether or not she should marry him.

Usually, when my sister makes up her mind, she jumps right into things. But this time, even after three months, she still couldn't make a decision. I suppose the idea of marriage filled her with dread and uncertainty.

WATASHI NO SUKINAHITO

わたしのすきなひと

So when I was in high school and she came to me for advice, I said to her, "Now, you should do the things only a single person can do. And once you get married, you should do the things only a married couple can do."

Now, of course, I wasn't married, so who was I to say something like that, but she seemed satisfied with my answer. And now, she is living happily in Osaka with a wonderful husband and her two girls—Mako and Utako.

On that happy note, The One I Love has come to an end. Thank you so much for staying with us on this journey through love. I still may know nothing when it comes to love, but if we ever have a chance to meet again, you can tell me all about it, okay?

WATASHI NO SUKINAHITO
わたしのすきなひと

We dedicate this book to all those we adore.

END

PLANNING AND PRESENTED BY CLAMP

THE ONE I LOVE
CLAMP
Newspaper—pirate Version
FINALLY, THE ONE I LOVE HAS BEEN COMPILED INTO THIS BOOK.
WITH THIS SERIES RUNNING EIGHT PAGES PER MONTH, I WAS BEGINNING TO WONDER WHEN IT WAS GONNA END.
TEA
CAFÉ AU LAIT
BUT SINCE THIS SERIES STARTED AT THE END OF 1993, IT'S BEEN ABOUT A YEAR AND A HALF.
しみじみ
RIGHT, RIGHT.
THIS WAS THE FIRST TIME THAT I ATTEMPTED A SERIES WHERE THE MAIN CHARACTER ISN'T A TWO HEAD-HEIGHT CHARACTER. PLUS, THE SERIES COMES WITH ESSAYS TOO, SO I WAS NERVOUS.
AND BESIDES, THIS WAS THE FIRST TIME I'VE DONE ILLUSTRATIONS FOR A STORY BY NANASE-CHAN...
It was nerve-wracking!
AREN'T YOU GLAD YOU GOT TO DRAW A LOT OF GIRLS?
It was fun being with the cat.

THIS TIME AROUND, WE WERE PUBLISHED IN A YOUNG WOMEN'S MAGAZINE, SO FOR CLAMP, WE WERE TARGETING A HIGHER AGE BRACKET.
YEAH, BUT EVEN THOUGH WE WERE TARGETING A BIT OLDER, MY ILLUSTRATIONS STILL MAKE THEM LOOK LIKE JUNIOR HIGH GIRLS.
Really an office lady who's dating a younger guy.
OH, BUT I THINK SHE LOOKS GOOD SERVING TEA IN A UNIFORM.
Somewhat...
I GOT MY COSTUME REFERENCES FROM "ANAN NON-NO OLIVE."
THE GIRL WHO APPEARED IN THE FIRST EPISODE WORE A GRUNGE OUTFIT.
Remember that?
HA HA! YOU WERE REALLY INTO GRUNGE BACK THEN.
Yeah, that's right, that's right.
BUT AFTER THAT, WE DIDN'T STICK TO ANY ONE STYLE.
THAT'S BECAUSE AT THAT AGE, WOMEN AREN'T SLAVES TO FASHION.
Making excuses.
BUT THAT'S JUST THE SETTING.
I mean the age.
THERE'S A DIFFERENCE BETWEEN CUTE OUTFITS THAT YOU'VE SEEN PEOPLE WEAR...
...AND CUTE OUTFITS THAT YOU DRAW.
At least nothing obvious at the time.
Good thing Chinese dresses were still in style.

A CHINESE-STYLE BLOUSE AND A SEE-THROUGH BAG AND SHOES.
WHAT'S THIS?
I JUST WANTED TO DRAW SOME GIRLS.
I WANTED TO KEEP CHANGING THEIR OUTFITS TO MAKE THEM LOOK PRETTY.
It's nice when you can keep doing that in a manga.
SPEAKING OF PATTERNS... IN EVERY CHAPTER IN THE PREVIEW PANELS, WE USED A DIFFERENT MOTIF EACH TIME. DID YOU CATCH IT?
くるーり
THAT'S RIGHT. ALTHOUGH DUE TO THE SIZE OF THE PICTURE I THINK MOST PEOPLE MISSED 'EM.
ぷるん
GIRLS (MOSTLY) AND ANIMALS...
Meow...
...WERE INCLUDED AS A RULE.
BUT IN ONE OF THE COLOR PANELS I FORGOT TO DRAW IN AN ANIMAL.
Heh heh. I forgot to take a picture
YOU FORGOT TO INCLUDE AN ANIMAL IN ONE OF THE TITLE PANELS TOO.

WELL, I HAD FUN WITH THIS SERIES, BEING ABLE TO DRAW SO MANY GIRLS.
GUYS WERE PRETTY MUCH JUST SUPPORTING PLAYERS.
YOU KNOW, GUYS ARE HARD TO DRAW, TOO.
THERE ARE ONLY SO MANY "GUY" HAIRSTYLES.
CLOTHES ARE A STANDARD ITEM, BUT THE OUTFITS HAVE TO MATCH THE CHARACTERS.
WHEN I DRAW A SALARYMAN IN A SUIT, HE STILL LOOKS LIKE A KID.
It's a harmonica salaryman.
This guy does really look like a kid.
I'D LIKE TO BE ABLE TO DRAW A TASTEFUL SALARYMAN.
Like a Sean Connery salaryman. Too cool...
A SENIOR SALARYMAN? MAYBE IN A DIFFERENT MAGAZINE.
Try again!
How about a Harrison Ford salaryman?
I THINK THERE ARE A LOT OF THINGS I NEED TO RECONSIDER.
NOBODY CAN GET IT PERFECT THE FIRST TIME. WE'LL WORK ON IT TOGETHER.
Ohh... I promise to work hard.
SO ANYWAY, ALL OF US AT CLAMP WILL STRIVE TO WORK TOGETHER AS ONE!!
Smirk.
Heh heh heh.
SO WE CAN BE MANGA-KA UNTIL WE'RE OLD AND GRAY?!
OF COURSE NOT!
Awooo!
END
spin spin spin!

The One I Love

Watashi No Sukinahito

Created by CLAMP

Translation - Ray Yoshimoto
Copy Editor - Hope Donovan
Retouch and Lettering - Abelardo Bigting
Production Artists - John Lo and James Lee
Cover Design - Anna Kernbaum

Editor - Nicole Monastirsky
Digital Imaging Manager - Chris Buford
Pre-Press Manager - Antonio DePietro
Production Managers - Jennifer Miller and Mutsumi Miyazaki
Art Director - Matt Alford
Managing Editor - Jill Freshney
VP of Production - Ron Klamert
President and C.O.O. - John Parker
Publisher and C.E.O. - Stuart Levy

A TOKYOPOP® Manga

TOKYOPOP Inc.
5900 Wilshire Blvd. Suite 2000
Los Angeles, CA 90036

E-mail: info@TOKYOPOP.com
Come visit us online at www.TOKYOPOP.com

ISBN: 1-59182-764-7

First TOKYOPOP printing: October 2004

10 9 8 7 6 5 4 3 2 1

Printed in the USA

TOKYOPOP®
SUKI™
A like story...
by CLAMP
T TEEN AGE 13+
©1999 CLAMP. ©2004 TOKYOPOP Inc. All Rights Reserved.
www.TOKYOPOP.com

TOKYOPOP®
新・春香伝
Legend of Chun Hyang™
FROM CLAMP
CREATORS OF CHOBITS & TOKYO BABYLON
A Brutal Tyrant...A Beautiful Warrior...A Legend In The Maki
T
TEEN AGE 13+
©1992 CLAMP. ©2004 TOKYOPOP Inc. All Rights Reserved.
www.TOKYOPOP.com

STOP!

This is the back of the book.
You wouldn't want to spoil a great ending!

This book is printed "manga-style," in the authentic Japanese right-to-left format. Since none of the artwork has been flipped or altered, readers get to experience the story just as the creator intended. You've been asking for it, so TOKYOPOP® delivered: authentic, hot-off-the-press, and far more fun!

DIRECTIONS

If this is your first time reading manga-style, here's a quick guide to help you understand how it works.

It's easy... just start in the top right panel and follow the numbers. Have fun, and look for more 100% authentic manga from TOKYOPOP®!

100% AUTHENTIC MANGA
品質第一公式商品